ONE LAST DROP

"Two more miles and we'll break into open tableland," Fargo said. "If we—"

The Trailsman never finished his sentence. The Ovaro, moving forward at a slow, steady trot, planted his left forefoot and then suddenly plummeted toward the ground.

Fargo, caught completely by surprise, jerked his feet from the stirrups. His first thought was that his stallion had stepped into a gopher hole, and Fargo didn't want his legs trapped when the Ovaro fell.

But this "hole," Fargo quickly realized when both of the Ovaro's forelegs were swallowed up, was a man-made pitfall trap. The leaf-covered framework of boughs collapsed, and Fargo pitched forward hard over his pommel—straight toward three pointed stakes smeared black with deadly poison!

D1024012

THE TRAILSMAN

#384

DIABLO
DEATH CRY

by

Jon Sharpe

A SIGNET BOOK

SIGNET
Published by the Penguin Group
Penguin Group (USA) LLC, 375 Hudson Street,
New York, New York 10014

USA | Canada | UK | Ireland | Australia | New Zealand | India | South Africa | China
penguin.com
A Penguin Random House Company

First published by Signet, an imprint of New American Library,
a division of Penguin Group (USA) LLC

First Printing, October 2013

The first chapter of this book previously appeared in *High Plains Massacre*, the
three hundred eighty-third volume in this series.

 REGISTERED TRADEMARK—MARCA REGISTRADA

ISBN 978-0-451-41951-4

Printed in the United States of America
10 9 8 7 6 5 4 3 2 1

The Trailsman

Beginnings . . . they bend the tree and they mark the man. Skye Fargo was born when he was eighteen. Terror was his midwife, vengeance his first cry. Killing spawned Skye Fargo, ruthless, cold-blooded murder. Out of the acrid smoke of gunpowder still hanging in the air, he rose, cried out a promise never forgotten.

The Trailsman they began to call him all across the West: searcher, scout, hunter, the man who could see where others only looked, his skills for hire but not his soul, the man who lived each day to the fullest, yet trailed each tomorrow. Skye Fargo, the Trailsman, the seeker who could take the wildness of a land and the wanting of a woman and make them his own.

The Southwest Trail (Texas and New Mexico), 1861—where Skye Fargo sets out to make a few easy dollars and gets caught in a deadly web of conspiracy and treason.

1

The words had plagued Skye Fargo's mind since he had headed south from Red River to start this new job: *Wait for what will come.*

That was how Hernando Quintana had ended his first dispatch to Fargo. And what eventually came was a new chamois pouch filled with five hundred dollars in gold double eagles—and a promissory note for five hundred more at the completion of the job.

That was way too much money. And Fargo had learned long ago that when men overpaid him, it generally meant he was going to be the meat that feeds the tiger.

Wait for what will come.

"The story of my life," Fargo muttered.

"The hell are you mumbling, Catfish?" demanded the man mountain blocking out the sun on Fargo's left. "Speak up like you own a pair!"

Fargo and his recently hired companion, Bill "Booger" McTeague, were riding through the flat saw grass country of the Gulf Coast in east Texas. On their left, the metallic blue water of the Gulf of Mexico stretched out to infinity, furling waves beating themselves into cotton foam as they crashed onto the white sand beach.

Fargo reined in his black-and-white pinto stallion and shaded his lake blue eyes with one hand, taking a careful squint ahead and behind. He sat tall in the saddle, a broad-shouldered, narrow-hipped, crop-bearded man dressed in fringed buckskins. A dust-darkened white hat left most of his weather-bronzed face in shadow.

"What I said," Fargo finally replied, "is that the two of us

1

will soon be up against it. The back of my neck has been tingling for the past hour."

"Pah!" Booger loosed a brown streamer into the knee-high grass. "Pull up your skirts, Nancy! All you jaspers with pretty teeth are squeamish. Why, this job is money for old rope. We may have to kill a Comanch or two, and p'r'aps a few Apaches will try to blow out our wicks, is all."

Fargo gigged the Ovaro forward again after loosening his Henry repeater in its saddle boot.

"We'll be hugging with red aborigines, all right," he said. "You can't avoid them on the southern route into California. And these Southwest tribes can't be bought off with tribute like the ones up north. Matter fact, we're being watched right now—and there's a tribe in this area, the Karankawas, known to be cannibals."

At this startling intelligence, Booger's head snapped toward Fargo. "No Choctaw here, Catfish. Is that the straight word?"

Fargo's lips twitched into a grin. Booger's moon face looked more curious than frightened. The shaggy giant was six feet five inches tall and weighed two hundred and eighty-five pounds. His prodigious bulk forced him to ride a saddle ox on long rides like this one. He was thick in the chest and waist, his arms bigger around the wrists than most brawny men were in the forearms. He wore a floppy hat and butternut-dyed shirt and trousers with knee-length elk-skin moccasins.

"It is," Fargo replied. "But it's not cannibals watching us, old son."

"Fargo, you double-poxed hound, I am not the lad for riddles. Who is it?"

Again the ominous words snapped in Fargo's mind like burning twigs: *Wait for what will come.*

"I don't have the foggiest notion in hell," he admitted. "But I suspect it's somebody who's been expecting us, and I doubt if he means to invite us to a cider party."

Booger threw back his head and howled like a wolf. "Faugh! A good set-to makes my pecker hard. Put a name to it and I will kill it. Nerve up, you little pipsqueak. Say! Old Booger used to whip an Overland swift wagon on the San Antonio Road. There is a fine whorehouse at Powder-horn.

We can get liquored up and plant our carrots before we even report to these dagos."

"Clean your ears or cut your hair. I think somebody's laying for us. No frippit and no carousing until we puzzle this deal out."

Booger looked mortally offended.

"Fargo, when did you become so old maidish? I do not require your permission to top a hot little senyoreeter."

"You do as long as you're working for me, you mammoth ape. I put you on the payroll because Quintana demanded the best driver I could find. But I *won't* take your damn guff."

"No need to get your bowels in an uproar. Gerlong there, Ambrose!" Booger called to his saddle ox. "G'long there, *whoop!*"

At first Fargo had been skeptical of Ambrose. But although the huge, placid beast could not move at a fast clip, he could cover twenty-four miles in four hours even in heavy sand. The Ovaro had quickly accepted the good-natured animal, and in any event the only alternative for a man of Booger's size was a conveyance and team.

Fargo's startling blue eyes stayed in constant scanning motion despite the flat, open terrain. He especially paid attention to the Ovaro's delicately veined ears. They were often the first indication of potential trouble.

Ten minutes passed in silence, each man alone with his thoughts. Then:

"This Espanish hombre," Booger said. "The hell's his name again?"

"Hernando Quintana."

"Is he one a' them whatchacallits—grandees?"

"Nah. He was a viceroy until the Mexican Revolution."

"The hell's a viceroy?"

The Ovaro's ears twitched. Eyes slitted against the bright sunlight, Fargo took another good squint around them.

"It's a fellow who governs a province for the Spanish king," he finally replied. "This one was in charge of Monterrey, Mexico. A lot of 'em were killed when the revolution broke out, but this Quintana escaped to New Orleans."

Booger grunted. He hawked up phlegm, spat, then said sarcastically, "Bully for him. Them garlics gripe my nuts.

It's them bastards that taught the featherheads to scalp and torture."

"Never mind the soapbox," Fargo said, watching the brisk gulf breeze ripple through the tall saw grass in waves. "Just keep a weather eye out for trouble. We're both hanging out here exposed like a set of dog balls."

"Teach your grandmother to suck eggs, nervous Nellie! Why, a titmouse couldn't sneak up on us in country this open and flat."

Fargo couldn't gainsay that. But years of frontier survival had taught him how danger sometimes gave the air a certain texture. And he felt that texture now—a galvanic charge like the one he sometimes felt just before a massive crack of thunder and lightning.

Booger gnawed off a corner of plug. When he had it juicing good, he parked it in his cheek and said, "Say, Catfish . . . will there be any women in this dago's party?"

"He mentioned his daughter."

"Ha-ho, ha-ho! A daughter, and he hires on the Trailsman? Oh, Lulu girl! You'll have her ankles behind her ears before next breakfast."

Fargo let out a long, fluming sigh. "Booger, you ain't got enough brains to have a headache. Now, you listen up: Spaniards are known for taking quick offense. I want you to mind your manners around them, hear? You keep a civil tongue in your head. And Christ sakes, *don't* be spying on the women when they bathe. That's a dangerous habit and will get you shot someday."

"Pipe down, you jay. Easy for you to say—you've seen more quiff than a midwife. Old Booger ain't had a woman in so long he's forgot what the gash that never heals looks like."

Fargo snorted. "Somebody get me a violin."

Within the next hour the two riders reached the northeast shore of Matagorda Bay. Powder-horn, a jumping-off settlement a few miles inland, marked the beginning of a good wagon road that had been well traveled since the army built it in 1849. Fargo was to join the Quintana party there.

They turned west onto a narrow trace that led past windswooped palm trees and gigantic live oaks draped in graygreen curtains of Spanish moss. Fargo considered this part of

Texas an extension of the Deep South but far more dangerous: law was scarce and gangs of ruthless *contrabandistas*
controlled the region, part of the smuggling operations that
flourished all along the western Gulf of Mexico.

The giant, spreading limbs overhead blocked much of the
sunlight, and the wide-boled trees themselves made for an
ambushers' paradise. The Ovaro, used to wide-open country
and good visibility, stutter-stepped nervously now and
then—like Fargo, he didn't take to being hemmed in.

Fargo had jerked his brass-framed Henry from its saddle
scabbard and now rode with it balanced across his left arm.
Booger, rocking sideways on his loose-skinned saddle ox,
kept his cap-and-ball Colt's Dragoon to hand.

"This place is heap bad medicine," he remarked. "Too
damn quiet, hey? No bird noises, no insect hum. Quiet as the
grave. Gives old Booger the fantods."

Fargo had noticed the same thing. The stillness was so
complete it seemed to scream.

Again, the unwelcome words nagged his memory like the
tag end of a song he hated but could not shake: *Wait for what
will come. . . . Wait. . . .*

The trace narrowed even more and Fargo gigged the
Ovaro ahead so the men could ride single file. A carpet of
leathery oak leaves covered the trace.

"Two more miles and we'll break into open tableland,"
Fargo said. "If we—"

The Trailsman never finished his sentence. The Ovaro,
moving forward at a slow, steady trot, planted his left forefoot and then suddenly plummeted toward the ground.

Fargo, caught completely by surprise, jerked his feet from
the stirrups. His first thought was that his stallion had
stepped into a gopher hole, and Fargo didn't want his legs
trapped when the Ovaro fell.

But this "hole," Fargo quickly realized when both of the
Ovaro's forelegs were swallowed up, was a man-made pitfall
trap. The leaf-covered framework of boughs collapsed, and
Fargo pitched forward hard over his pommel—straight
toward three pointed stakes smeared black with deadly
poison!

2

One reason Skye Fargo had cheated death so often was his hair-trigger reactions at those critical moments when other men tended to freeze up.

The instant Fargo crashed into the pitfall, things started happening ten ways a second. The Ovaro managed to avoid the stakes, twisting fast and scrambling out to safety before his hind legs entered the trap.

As for his master—even as Fargo flew over the pommel, he managed to deftly swing his long Henry rifle out in front of him. He didn't have the luxury of planning his movement—it was pure reflex and athleticism.

In the fraction of a second that he was airborne, Fargo somehow got the Henry into position with both hands on the walnut stock. The very moment it slammed muzzle-first into the pit, Fargo literally vaulted over the stakes.

He barely managed to clear the pitfall and crash down safe on the opposite side.

"Well, God kiss me!" Booger exclaimed in awe behind him. He heaved himself off Ambrose's back. "Still sassy, Tumbledown Dick?"

Fargo, heart still pounding like a Pawnee war drum, rose a bit unsteadily to his feet. He caught the nervous Ovaro by the bridle reins.

"Still sassy," he replied. "But that was paring the cheese mighty close to the rind, old son."

"The hell *is* that shit?" Booger demanded, staring at the shiny black gunk on the stakes.

Fargo picked up his hat, slapped the dust from it, and clapped it back on his head.

"I don't know for sure, but I've seen it before. It's extracted from plants. Sure as cats fighting, it will air-choke a man quicker'n you can gobble a biscuit. Settle down, old war-horse," he added, patting the Ovaro's withers.

"This pit's fresh dug," Booger said. "But if it was the work of road agents, how's come they ain't shot us to chair stuffings by now?"

"There's nobody waiting around here," Fargo replied. "My pinto would have alerted. This wasn't the work of curly wolves looking for swag—since nobody knows I hired you, it was meant to kill me. Like I said, somebody knows I'm coming and wants to stop me."

"H'ar, now! Fargo, you are the world-beatingest man. Every rain shower ain't meant to get just *you* wet."

"Maybe," Fargo said, not sounding too convinced.

When the Ovaro had been gentled, Fargo checked the cinches and latigos. Then he turned the stirrup and swung up onto the hurricane deck.

"There could be another pitfall," he said as he tightened the reins. "Crowd the side of the trail as much as you can and be ready to tug rein."

"Crowd the side of the trail," Booger repeated in a scornful voice, "and be ready to tug rein. Fargo, is your brain any bigger than your pee hole? There is no bit in Ambrose's mouth. You call this reins?"

Booger shook the tough leather thong in his left hand. Saddle oxen could not be controlled by bits, so a short, strong stick had been forced through the cartilage of the nose. The thong was tied to each end of it. Because of the extreme tenderness of the nose, an ox could thus be steered and managed, but somewhat clumsily.

"Prob'ly won't matter," Fargo said. "The pitfall will be dug for a horse, and Ambrose is too big to fall in. Hell, *you're* too big."

"Large and in charge," Booger boasted as the two men again bore west.

They rode silently, the only sounds the creak of saddle leather and the Ovaro snuffling. In new country a horse was nervous until it had smelled the ground sufficiently, so Fargo gave the stallion his head.

"Happens somebody *is* trying to put the quietus on us,"

7

Booger spoke up from behind Fargo, picking up the conversational thread from earlier. "You think it's this pepper-gut Quintana?"

"Makes no sense. I just finished a job as a payroll guard for Colonel Oglethorpe up at Fort Smith. He's from New Orleans and says Quintana has lived there since just after the Mexer Revolution. I've never met Quintana, so why would he try to plant me?"

"And why not? Fargo, you sheep-humping, chicken-plucking bachelor of the saddle, many is the night *I've* prayed you into the ground, pretty teeth and all. Gerlong there, Ambrose! *Whoop!*"

A few minutes later Booger again broke the preternatural silence.

"Fargo, I been thinking—"

"There you go, exaggerating again."

Booger gave him the evil eye. "I see you've tired of eating solid food. Anyhow, it makes no sense, Catfish. The Espanish are well settled in New Orleans. Why would this here viceroy just pull up stakes and head for the Bear Flag Republic? The garlics ain't so welcome there since the Mex'can War."

"He told me in his dispatch that his doctors ordered it—something about the 'noxious miasma' in New Orleans being bad for his lungs."

"Aye, it is a foul, stinking place. But a man need not cut his arm off at the elbow just to cure a hangnail, hey? He could move upriver to Memphis and not have to face the painted savages of Texas and New Mexico Territory—nor the Mex'can freebooters."

Fargo shrugged. "Each man to his own gait. Oglethorpe says the viceroy has been at loose ends since his wife was killed by yellow fever. Sometimes a man just wants to get as far away as he can from bad memories."

Booger made a farting noise with his lips. "Yes, by watching his daughter get raped by twenty Kiowa bucks before they raise her hair? Ain't *he* the sensitive son of a bitch! To old Booger, it don't quite cipher."

"It does seem a mite queer," Fargo admitted. "Then again,

he's got us on the payroll, two men with brass onions, to get him through. And there's other armed men with him."

Fargo heaved a sigh of relief when they finally broke free of the dense tree cover without further incident and rode out onto the broad, grassy expanse west of Matagorda Bay. Powderhorn, an outfitting camp for the less traveled southern route to the west, known as the Southwest Trail, lay below the low ridge they were following, a sprawl of tents, dugouts, livestock corrals, mercantiles, saloons, and a large wagon yard with a smithy.

"Damn your bones, Fargo," Booger groused, casting a wistful eye toward the settlement. "Just a brief stop to dip our beaks?"

"Nix on that. That pitfall was our warning. Once you get a snoot full of who-shot-John in you, you'll seek out the comfort of a soiled dove. And the best time to kill a man is when he's taking a crap or in the heat of the rut. The Quintana party is just a mile past Powder-horn, so let's make our report."

"Satan's pushing me from behind, Fargo! Take pity on old Booger."

"Put it away from your mind for now. Remember, this is not the Oregon Trail—there will be good stores and settlements along this route."

"Pah!" Booger spat a brown streamer into the grass and scowled with frustration. "Fargo, you son of a motherless goat! I oughter shoot you, take your gold, and go on a three-day carouse. You've turned into a bluenosed temperance biddy, Goddamn it!"

Fargo transformed his face into a mask of piety and replied in a pulpit tone, "Now, now, brother Booger—God's last name isn't Damn it."

Fargo found the Quintana party right where he was told they would be, but his reception turned out to be an unpleasant surprise.

The new arrivals stopped about fifty yards out, surveying the staging area.

Booger, a veteran knight of the ribbons who had whipped

the best Concord coaches for the Overland Stage Company, loosed an appreciative whistle.

"Christmas crackers! Wouldja glom that fancy rig I'll be driving, Fargo! Thoroughbraces *and* springs! I ain't never seen the like."

"It's some pumpkins," Fargo agreed, admiring the jet-black japanned coach shining like new tar in the coppery late-afternoon sunshine. "The outfitter must still be down there, too. Look at all the livestock and provisions."

Everything was in a great stirring and to-do. A temporary rope corral had been set up, crowded with horses and mules. Wooden crates of supplies were stacked everywhere among fodder wagons, high-walled freight wagons, and two "mud wagons," light, cheap coaches without doors. What truly surprised Fargo, however, was the large number of mostly young men, most of them evidently Spanish or Mexican.

Three of whom now rode out toward Fargo and Booger.

"Cut off my nuts and call me Squeaky," Booger said. "Are them bellhops?"

"Spanish soldiers," Fargo said, his tone wondering. "Two officers and a sergeant. This deal ain't what I expected, old son."

One of the soldiers rode slightly ahead of the others on a coal black Arabian wearing a fancy, silver-trimmed saddle. The officer reined in about ten feet from the dusty, trail-worn frontiersmen. The metal facing on his tall shako hat glinted in the sun.

"My name is Captain Diego Salazar of Seville, *a sus ordenes.*" He greeted Fargo with stiff formality. "You must be the scout named Fargo?"

His dismissive tone—as if Fargo were the lowest menial—made the Trailsman immediately dislike the smug son of a bitch. Fargo took in the neat, slender, mustachioed Spaniard. He wore a well-cut frogged jacket and tight, gold-braided trousers tucked into shiny boots that almost covered his calves. His hard, tight-lipped mouth was straight as a seam.

"Yeah, I'm Fargo," he replied, adding in his mild way, "I'm a mite curious, Captain. What are uniformed foreign soldiers doing on sovereign American soil?"

Salazar seemed annoyed, as if the question were impertinent.

"We are retained by His Excellency, don Hernando Quintana, viceroy of Monterrey. We have letters of marque from Governor Miro of Louisiana that identify us as soldiers of the Spanish Crown."

Fargo's eyes shifted to the two uniformed soldiers sitting their saddles behind Salazar. The captain noticed this.

"Lieutenant Juan Aragon," he said curtly, "and my orderly, Sergeant Rivera."

Aragon had a disapproving face with dead, glass-button eyes. The sergeant was stout and brutish-looking. Neither man noticed the introduction—they were staring with a mixture of contempt and awe at Booger and Ambrose.

"*This* is the driver you hired?" Salazar asked Fargo.

"Does Raggedy Ann have a patched ass?" Booger spoke up, his moon face reddening with anger. "Booger McTeague here, a true-blue, blown-in-the-bottle, man-eating—"

"Caulk up, knothead," Fargo cut in. He didn't like this arrogant trio, either, but he was diplomatic when large sums of money were in the mix.

Booger's Irish temper, however, made him quick to rile and slow to cool off.

"Seems to me," he told Fargo, "like these three sons of de Soto are surprised to see you above the horizon, Skye, y'unnerstan'? Like just maybe they was expecting you to have a little accident back along the trail."

"These *norteamericanos*," Lieutenant Aragon spoke up, "need to be taught a lesson about respect for their betters, *verdad, Capitan*? Most especially *el gordo* here, who is an ass riding on an ox."

"Why, you greaser pipsqueak! You're plucking the wrong bird, soldier. Fargo, I don't palaver the lingo too good—the hell's a gordo?"

Both of the officers wore what Fargo sarcastically called cheese knives—gold-hilt sabers, the blades thirty-three inches of deadly Toledo steel. They were virtually worthless on the frontier, where a weapon like the Arkansas toothpick in Fargo's boot sheath could kill much quicker. But the Volcanic repeating sidearms in their flap holsters were not for show.

"Simmer down," Fargo ordered, placing a hand on

Booger's massive shoulder when he started to slide to the ground. "You started it, mouth."

Salazar looked at Fargo, everything in his face smiling except the eyes. "Yes, we must all 'simmer down' as you say. His Excellency expects all of us to work together."

Fargo glanced closer at Rivera, the hulking brute of a sergeant. His eyes had the burning luminosity of an insane fanatic. He wore a machete in a shoulder scabbard—definitely no cheese knife. Fargo knew that short, curved blade was capable of severing a man's spine like a cane stalk.

"Sounds jake to me," Fargo finally replied. "I'm here to do a good job and make money."

"Don Hernando will want to speak with you soon," Salazar added. "But he is a—how do you say?—fastidious man with a sensitive nose. I suggest you both bathe first. You will find hot food in the camp."

All three men cast one last, mocking glance at the shabby giant perched on an ox, then reined their mounts around and rode back to the staging camp.

"Come back again when you can't stay so long, Sanchos," Booger told their retreating backs.

He spat into the grass and aimed a withering glance at Fargo. " 'Sounds jake to me.' Trailsman, get to the sewing lodge. That skull-faced, cock-chafing Aragon called me a gordo! And that Salazar—why, he prac'ly lopped off your nuts!"

"You listen to me, you big ugly ape, and you listen good. There's a damn good chance you're right about that pitfall, savvy?"

Booger cocked his head, confused. "Huh? Then how's come—"

"Because I'm not a thick-skulled, hot-jawing fool like you, that's why. Booger, a man has to wade in slow until he knows how deep the water is. There's a camp full of dons down there. Sure, we could've blown all three of those whip dicks outta their saddles, and then you tell me—how fast could you have skedaddled on Ambrose?"

Booger showed the first signs of contrition. "I take your drift."

"All right. Right now we're the hind-tit boys. We bide our

time, keep our eyes and ears open, and figure this deal out. *You* put a tether on that tongue."

They gigged their mounts into motion and headed toward the camp.

"You know, Catfish," Booger opined, "that Sergeant Rivera didn't say one damn word, but I make him out the most dangersome of the three. Did you *see* that fucker's crazy eyes? He's an easy-go killer, all right."

"Yeah. He's got that Latin look—pig Latin."

3

Both men headed toward the makeshift corral.

"Hey-up, boys!" a friendly voice greeted them. "The name is Bitch Creek McDade, but most folks just call me Bitch except in mixed company. I'm the wrangler for this glorious outfit."

At first Fargo thought a ghost might be speaking. Then he saw the speaker emerge from amid a milling tangle of mules. He was short but descended from big-boned Ulster stock, the same tough, hard-knit men who filled the ranks of America's police forces and army barracks.

Fargo reined in and swung down from the saddle. "Hey-up yourself. Most fellows wouldn't take kindly to being called Bitch."

The sturdy redhead tossed back his head and laughed. "Yeah, but it cuts down on dustups. See, when a man's name is Bitch, why, the insult is already built into it. No need to call him any more names. Say! That is one crackerjack stallion, friend!"

He glanced at Booger, just then sliding to the ground, and gave him a quick size-up.

"So I finally meet Paul Bunyan and his blue ox. Big fella, I can see why you need to straddle an ox. Say, you're big enough to fight cougars with a shoe."

"I had a cougar for breakfast," Booger boasted. "Didn't take a shoe off, neither."

Fargo threw the bridle, then slipped the bit and loosed the cinch. "Bitch, meet your fellow Irishman Booger McTeague, the best damn reinsman who never rolled an Overland stage. I'm Skye Fargo."

"Pleased. I've heard about you, Mr. Fargo. My boss knows

14

you—he's the outfitter for this fandango. That's him over there—the skinny, baldheaded rake counting crates."

Fargo glanced where McDade pointed.

"Sure, that's Jerome Helzer. He used to run the sutler store out at Fort Union. I see he stole enough legem pone from the army to set himself up in business."

McDade laughed again as he pulled Fargo's saddle. "For a surety. He's got money to toss at the birds now. He hired out me and Deke Lafferty, the cook, to this Quintana gent."

"Bitch, you don't sound overjoyed about it," Booger chimed in.

McDade shrugged a shoulder. "Ah, the money's good, I s'pose. But these Spaniards seem a might clannish. The old man, Quintana, is full of himself and talks like a book, but he seems a pretty good sort."

McDade glanced quickly around, then lowered his voice. "I'm clemmed, though, if I can figure out all these damned soldiers. I see you boys just met Salazar, Aragon, and that greasy-looking Rivera. Those three are the topkicks. Sweet outfit, huh?"

"Topkicks?" Fargo repeated. "You mean there's more soldiers?"

"Hell yes. Those three are the only ones in uniform but most of the others"—McDade hooked a thumb toward the camp—"are soldiers in mufti, or leastways I'd wager on it. I've heard Salazar call some of them by their rank."

"Interesting," was all Fargo said. But Booger was not so discreet.

"Fargo, this shit's for the birds. I don't take kindly to a man who pisses down my back and tells me it's raining. You told me some rich old dago toff is moving out to California for his health. Seems to me 'His Excellency' is sailing under false colors."

"No need to have a conniption," Fargo said. "This Quintana fellow was pretty high up in the Spanish government. When the Mexican Revolution sparked up, the viceroys were hanged, shot, or managed to escape. There's still a kill-or-capture order on them, and you know damn well the Mexicans don't always stay on their side of the border. It's no big mystery why he might have soldiers around him."

"Pah! Happens all that's so, Catfish, why didn't he just hie on back to Spain where he'd be safe?"

Fargo tugged at his short chin whiskers, mulling that over.

"That's a tough nut to crack," he admitted.

"Helzer told me," McDade chipped in, "that the viceroy married an actress from New Orleans. They had a daughter before his wife died—maybe he didn't leave because his wife wouldn't leave New Orleans. Speaking of his daughter . . ."

The wrangler pointed with his chin toward a huge tent in the middle of the bustling camp. Fargo watched a striking young woman, wearing a low-cut emerald green dress with velvet-trimmed cuffs, emerge through the fly. Her jeweled tiara caught the rays of a descending sun and seemed to flash into flame.

"Senorita Miranda Quintana," McDade said in an almost reverent tone. "Boyos, she is *some*. Pretty as four aces. A reg'lar Venus de Milo. But us working stiffs have got our orders from Captain Salazar—we can't talk to her, stand close to her, nor even make eye contact with her."

Booger snorted. "Well, Fargo, you're a hound. The dago didn't say you couldn't *lie* close to her. If you don't look at her or speak to her, p'r'aps you can still screw her, eh?"

Fargo's eyes lingered on her as Miranda gazed around the camp. Her gaze met his. She watched him for a few long moments before demurely covering half her face with a palmetto fan and retreating into the tent.

McDade whistled. "I'll be jiggered, Mr. Fargo! I think that little gal's got a sweet tooth for you already. It's likely she knew you were coming—everybody else did."

"Bless her heart," Fargo said. "But that touching little scene just now didn't go unnoticed. Stand by for the blast, boys. Booger, keep a stopper on your gob, hear me?"

Captain Salazar, Lieutenant Aragon, and Sergeant Rivera were striding purposefully toward the corral. Salazar's face was grim with disapproval.

"Look at them talking magpies," Booger muttered. "They're keeping step with each other. I wunner if they all piss at the same times like cows do."

"Senor Fargo," Salazar said as the trio drew near. "You

will find hot water and tubs one hundred yards north of camp. I suggest you and your friend avail yourselves of them."

"We were planning to," Fargo said. "But I didn't realize it was an order."

"And if it were?"

"Then you and me would have us a little problem."

Sergeant Rivera spoke up for his superior. "*El Capitan* does not give orders to civilians. If they do not follow his . . . suggestions, it falls to me to persuade them. *Entiende?*"

A hairy-knuckled hand patted the sheath of his machete.

"Sure, I understand," Fargo replied cheerfully. "Persuasion I don't mind."

"I did not mention to you," Salazar said, "how things are between His Excellency's daughter and myself. You see, we have . . . an understanding. We are not yet formally engaged to be wed, but we soon will be."

"Congratulations," Fargo said. "She looks like a very pretty girl."

Salazar's hard seam of mouth tightened even more. "*Claro.* I mention this only because your reputation for— how do you say?—amorous adventures is widely known. It would be unfortunate for you if you do not . . . control your usual impulses."

To Fargo all of this was just chicken shit and he ignored it. Something more important was on his mind. Whether in warfare or at times like this, he followed a useful credo: *Always mystify, mislead, and surprise.*

Right now he opted for surprise.

"Tell me, Captain," he said, "would you know anything about a pitfall somebody dug on the trail to Powder-horn?"

Clearly Salazar had not expected such a question. "A pitfall?" he repeated, annoyed.

"Yeah, you know . . . a hole in the ground that's covered up so that a horse and rider fall into it? This one also had poisoned stakes in it."

Fargo had learned to spot a liar, even a good one. But Salazar looked genuinely puzzled. Fargo's eyes slanted toward Aragon. The lieutenant watched him from a sullen deadpan, the dead glass-button eyes registering nothing.

As for Rivera—that slight twitching of his lips might or might not have revealed guilt.

"No one here has plans to kill you," Salazar said irritably. "His Excellency sent for you to guide this expedition, and I do not impede his wishes. But, of course, your own willful, reckless behavior could endanger you. Remember what I told you."

The lake blue eyes that women found so intriguing now went hard and cold, as did the rest of Fargo's face.

"Take it easy, *muchachos*, all three of you," Fargo said in a low, toneless voice. "With me it's live and let live until it's kill or be killed. I will not abide a threat."

Fargo flexed his right hand, which lay against his holster. Salazar tried to stare him down but was the first to avert his eyes.

"You are confusing advice with a threat," he said. "*Vamanos, amigos*," he added, and the three men turned and walked away.

"Criminey, Fargo," McDade said, backhanding sweat from his freckled brow, "I thought certain sure we were about to have a cartridge session."

Booger cursed and swiped a hand across his lips, showing Fargo fresh blood. "See that, long-shanks? See what comes of putting a muzzle on old Booger? Why, I damn near bit clear through my lip. 'Persuasion I don't mind.' Why—"

"Bottle it." Fargo cut him off. "A wise man puts no foot down until there's a solid place to bear it."

"Pee doodles! These—"

Fargo raised a hand to silence him. "I said turn off the tap. We'll be huggin' with those soldier boys soon enough, I expect, but we're up against a cold deck here until we size this deal up and see which way the wind sets. Right now I'm gonna say howdy to Helzer, and then me and you are gonna have that bath we've been advised to have. We are a mite whiffy, old son."

"No, I didn't build that fine coach, Skye," Jerome Helzer, the outfitter from Powder-horn, answered Fargo's query. "Innit a little honey, though? He sent it by steamer from New Orleans to Steamboat Springs. Finest conveyance I've ever seen."

"Aye," Booger agreed, "and I've seen some of the finest. The queen of England herself would be proud to ride in that rig."

"Those wheels," Helzer added, tapping one with the toe of his boot, "are made from Osage orange wood, the same wood Kiowas use to fashion their bows. They will shrink very little and seldom require repairing. And they've been kiln dried to stand up to desert air."

Booger whistled. "Crikes! Look at the running gearing—the ends of all the bolts have been riveted."

"Is that good?" Fargo asked.

"Damn smart," Helzer replied. "Most carriage accidents happen when nuts fall off the bolts. This viceroy may dress in silks and pinch snuff, but he's had some top-notch advice about conveyances."

Booger grabbed the hoist bar and heaved himself onto the box. "Well, I'm a Dutchman! This is a lazy-back spring seat of cushioned leather!" he exclaimed. "My piles will feel neglected."

"That's nothing," Helzer said. "There's a big oaken water tank built in under that seat."

Booger stood and lifted the seat. "Christmas crackers! Why, if it was filled with whiskey—"

"That's the queer part of it," Helzer said. "When I offered to fill it with water, the old Spaniard nixed it. Said he could not afford the extra weight. But, Skye, it's only going to be him and two women riding, and he's hitching *eight* mules to that rig."

"Eight?" Fargo repeated. "For three passengers? Granted, Booger is a big grizz. But a mule is a strong puller—most of the range is flat, and six would be more than plenty."

"Sure, that's what I told him. But since he bought the mules from me, I didn't argue the point. I'm not the kind to shoot a hole in my own canoe."

"Eight mules," Fargo mused aloud, "and he won't fill the water tank, huh? Say, Booger, hop on down a minute."

"Hop a cat's tail. Old Booger likes this seat. I think I'll sleep on it. Hell, I might even marry it and sire a tribe of little baby stools."

"Hop down, you demented circus monkey," Fargo insisted. "I want to check on something."

Cursing, Booger climbed down. Fargo tucked at the knees to study the nearside wheels closer. "Huh. Booger, you're the expert here. I know this coach is resting on thick grass, but should it be cutting in that deep when it's standing empty?"

Booger and Helzer studied the wheels.

"Ha-ho, ha-ho!" Booger finally said. "Fargo, you may have the pretty teeth of a gal-boy, but also a keen eye. This is a sturdy rig, right enough, but it's cutting too deep."

"False bottom?" Helzer asked. "Maybe guns?"

"Guns don't seem likely," Fargo gainsaid. "They can be hauled openly with a two-dollar transit permit so long as they're not sold to the tribes."

"Quintana doesn't strike me as a *contrabandista*," Helzer said. "He—"

Booger interrupted in a low voice. "Lookit that pepper-gut scuttling toward us, boys—he looks as nervous as a long-tailed cat in a roomful of rocking chairs. He's been glomming us close."

"Senors," called out one of the young men Bitch Creek McDade suspected was a soldier in mufti. "His Excellency prefers that his personal conveyance not be disturbed."

"Dis-goddamn-*sturbed*? Just an ever-lovin' minute here, Sancho," Booger protested. "*I'm* the jasper who'll be whipping that coach."

The Spaniard wore the rope sandals and white cotton shirt and trousers of a *bracero* or common worker. But enough daylight remained for Fargo to notice a hard, contemptuous glint to his eyes. However, like most men with an ounce of sense, he was intimidated by the scowling, moon-faced giant looming over him like Judgment Day.

"*Como no,*" he said politely. "Of course, but His Excel—"

"Pah!" Booger spat into the grass. "Give over with this 'His Excellency' shit! I'm—"

"Chuck the flap jaw," Fargo snapped.

Fargo straightened to his full six feet. "Never mind this big gasbag," he told the young man. "We were just admiring the craftsmanship of your boss's rig. By the way, soldier, what's your rank?"

"I am . . . that is, I have no rank, senor. I have never been a soldier. I was a worker on don Hernando's sugarcane plantation."

"My mistake. Let's go have a hot bath, Booger, then stoke our bellies. I'm so hungry my backbone is rubbing against my rib cage."

"That garlic is a damn liar, Skye," Booger muttered as they walked off. "He's a soldier, right enough. And I'll eat my flap hat if that fine coach ain't got a false bottom."

"The way you say," Fargo agreed. "But so what? We ain't star packers. The pay is good, and we have no proof anybody is breaking any laws. Besides, neither one of us is a scrubbed angel. We've broke our share of laws, too. Whatever's in that coach is none of our picnic—leastways, not yet."

"Why, that's so, ain't it?" Booger agreed. "But old Booger still thinks we will have to put some men below the horizon before this trip is behind us."

"Lead *will* fly," Fargo agreed. And again the ominous words occurred to him unbidden: *Wait for what will come.*

4

As night drew her sable curtain over the east Texas saw grass country, Fargo and Booger enjoyed a long, hot soak in tubs made from whiskey barrels sawn in half. Booger eventually got stuck and Fargo nearly herniated himself prying him loose. Then they searched out the trail cook, Deke Lafferty, who obligingly warmed up beef and biscuits for the two new arrivals. Bitch Creek McDade, the affable wrangler, joined them for coffee.

"Fargo," McDade said, "I gave your stallion a good rub-down and took the currycomb to him before I grained him good. I checked his feet, too. I used a hoof pick to pry a few small stones loose, and all his shoes are tight. Booger, Ambrose got plenty of fodder."

"'Preciate it," Fargo said.

"Deke, them eats was tolerable good," Booger told the cook, picking his teeth with a horseshoe nail. "But this coffee . . . faugh! It is a vile concoction—too thin to chew and too thick to swallow."

"You're the only one bitching about it," Deke shot back. "This is whatcha call an all-purpose libation. It loosens up the bowels, cures hangovers, and makes a good horse liniment. And so long as you keep it away from an open flame, it's safe."

Lafferty was a thin, sallow man with a soup-strainer mustache and a mouthful of teeth like crooked yellow gravestones. He was around thirty with one of the oddest builds Fargo had ever seen: a strong torso on bandy legs so that he looked like a cabinet mounted on two poles.

"Never mind this big ugly flea hive, Deke," Fargo said. "He'd stand in a bread line and demand toast."

Deke took in Booger's impressive size. "Well, he'd *get* toast from me. 'At sumbitch is a big grizz, ain't he? He ain't a man—he's a county."

Jerome Helzer, the outfitter, had returned to Powder-horn. Fargo marveled at the stores and provisions Hernando Quintana had laid by for the journey. Bacon had been packed in strong sacks of a hundred pounds each; likewise flour had been packed in stout double canvas sacks. Sugar was well secured in gutta-percha. Desiccated, or dried, vegetables, almost equal when boiled to the taste of fresh, were stacked in compact tins. Men of the U.S. Army called them "desecrated vegetables" and "bailed hay," but Fargo was partial to them.

Pemmican, which kept fresh for months at a time, filled several large bags made from animal hides. Several dozen bushels of parched corn would feed men and horses over a long haul. There were also plentiful supplies of coffee, salt, and saleratus for making bread.

"You boys meet the viceroy yet?" McDade inquired as he blew on his coffee. The three men sat cross-legged around Deke's cooking fire.

"We'll look him up soon as we eat," Fargo replied. "I notice this bunch keeps picket guards outside the camp. You boys noticed any trouble?"

"Me and Bitch just got here yestiddy," Deke replied. "Ain't been no lead chucking nor nothin', but Diego Salazar and them two soldier sidekicks of his seem a mite nerve-jangled—wound up tighter than an eight-day clock. Like mebbe they're expectin' a set-to."

"What's your size-up of those three, Bitch?" Fargo pressed McDade.

"I'm no frontiersman like you, Fargo," McDade replied. "But I got enough sense not to drink downstream from the herd. *All* these Spanish gazabos strike me as a queer lot who belong in cities."

Fargo rose, rinsed his tin fork and plate in a wreck pan set up on two sawhorses, then wiped his hands on his buckskin trousers.

"All right, old son," he said to Booger, "let's go palaver with our employer. I haven't even seen him yet."

"See *him*? Pah! I would like to see more of his daughter. Deke, where do the women bathe?"

"Don't answer that, Deke," Fargo spoke up quickly. "Damn you, Booger, I told you not to start that shit with this bunch."

"Ah? You had no objections, pearly teeth, that night when old Booger showed you a peephole so's you could spy on that actress Kathleen Barton."

"Yeah, until you got all het up and crashed through the wall and knocked her outta the tub."

Both men laughed at the memory.

Deke looked flabbergasted. "You two seen Kathleen Barton, America's Sweetheart, nekked?"

"Oh, that was nothing, Catfish," Booger said, warming to his theme. "We seen her diddling herself while she cried out Fargo's name—"

"Your mouth runs like a whoopewill's ass," Fargo cut in, his tone laced with disgust. "C'mon. And keep a tether on your tongue."

Both men headed toward the huge tent at the center of camp. Torches had been lit all around the camp, and their sawing flames threw grotesque shape-changing shadows. Too damn many torches, in Fargo's opinion. The entire area was lit up almost as bright as day—a fact he didn't appreciate after that near miss with the pitfall earlier.

Hard upon that thought, Fargo felt tingling needle points on the back of his neck. It seemed as if the loud and bustling camp had suddenly grown quiet—too quiet.

"Booger, I'm thinking—"

For the second time that day Fargo never finished his sentence. A hammering racket of gunfire suddenly broke the stillness, and Fargo heard bullets snapping past his ears—a few so dangerously close he felt the wind rip from them.

"Kiss the ground!" he shouted, diving forward.

Unfortunately for Fargo, he and Booger dived for the exact same spot, and Fargo landed first. The air exploded from his lungs when nearly three hundred pounds landed on top of him like an anvil.

Bullets continued to thicken the air all around them, but suddenly Fargo was more worried about being crushed to death than shot.

"Off!" he managed to rasp out. "Get . . . *off*!"

"The hell *you* crying about?" Booger riposted. "No bullet can touch you now."

Fargo was on the verge of blacking out from oxygen deprivation. Suddenly, as abruptly as a door slamming shut, the firing ceased. Booger rolled off Fargo just before the Trailsman would have passed out.

Fargo, gasping like a fish in the bottom of a boat, heard distant shouts in Spanish—the perimeter guard, he guessed. A moment later Booger jerked him onto unsteady legs.

"That was no random volley, Catfish," Booger said, shaking Fargo back to his senses. "Them lead whistlers was aimed right at us!"

Fargo, still fighting for a full breath, only nodded.

"Either of you hit?" Bitch Creek McDade demanded, hurrying toward the two men.

"*This* little schoolgirl is breathless with fright," Booger scoffed. "P'r'aps she has even pissed her petticoats."

Deke Lafferty joined them. "Boys, I cal'late they was at least thirty shots fired."

He lowered his voice and added, "Christ only knows who done the lead chucking. Plenty of sons of Coronado out there."

Nobody saw Captain Diego Salazar until he spoke up. "You will remove that slander of the Spanish Crown, *cocinero*, or I will remove your tongue."

"Get off your high horse, Salazar," Fargo said, finding his voice with an effort. "You're on American soil now. Deke doesn't have to crawfish to you."

Salazar, his disapproving mouth wire-tight now, turned his attention to Fargo. "I advised don Hernando not to hire you. Trouble, it is said, follows you like an afternoon shadow. *You* have brought this trouble to our camp, Fargo. And I advise all of you *norteamericanos* to stop insulting us with your baseless accusations."

"Nobody accused you of anything. Deke only pointed out the obvious, that you've got plenty of armed 'plantation workers' out there. I'm warning you right now, and I don't chew my cabbage twice: If I find out you're behind these sneak attacks, I'm gonna cut you open from neck to nuts."

"It is indeed a pleasure to finally meet you, Senor Fargo," Hernando Quintana, former viceroy of Monterrey, Mexico, said in his cultured baritone. "One reads about the Trailsman in many newspapers and magazines. 'A promptitude of action' is how one writer explains your survival."

"Those ink slingers," Fargo said, "are more interested in selling bunkum for profit than in sticking to the facts."

Quintana smiled. "A man must admire a hero who does not sound his own trumpet. Still, I certainly wish your reception had been much less violent."

Quintana was a distinguished, silver-haired man in his sixties. The corners of his eyes crinkled like old shoe leather when he smiled. Despite his obvious politeness and dignified bearing, he could barely keep from staring at Fargo's huge and rustic companion, who seemed to fill at least half of the tent.

Fargo said, "This ugly mange pot is your driver, William 'Booger' McTeague. In seven years with Overland, he's never rolled a coach or lost a passenger. I'm not sure if it's his skill or his weight."

"As for weight," Booger chimed in, "your fine rig out there has plenty."

Quintana tugged at his goatee, watching the big reinsman closely. "How do you mean, sir?"

Fargo caught Booger's eye and sent him a warning.

"Why, I meant only that is a solid conveyance, to be sure. Heavy osage wood and iron castings . . ."

Quintana was not alone inside the commodious, comfortable tent. Miranda Quintana, seated in a canvas camp chair, had been watching Fargo with a quiet intensity.

"Gentlemen," Quintana said, "certainly you have noticed my daughter. Miranda's mother—*en paz descanza*, may she rest in peace—was an American *actriz*, much younger than I. Thus, you see, she combines the traits of the American and Spanish bloodlines to superlative effect."

"Oh, she caps the climax, all right," Booger ventured, and Miranda, still watching Fargo from languid dark berry eyes, smiled demurely.

"This other beauty," Quintana added gallantly, "is Katrina Robles, her duenna."

This news surprised Fargo. A duenna was supposed to be a much older woman who chaperoned a younger woman. But Katrina was still on the friendly side of thirty. The black lace mantilla she wore over her head could not disguise her pretty face and full, sultry lips.

"Senor Fargo," Quintana said, "this long journey ahead is terra incognita for me and the ladies. But I am told that no man in the United States or the American territories knows it better than you do. We are fortunate to have you as our guide."

"To be honest, sir," Fargo admitted, "I'm a mite curious as to why you folks didn't take the northern trail from St. Joe. It's rougher terrain, but there's greater safety in numbers."

"For one thing, I was informed, by an experienced wagon conductor, that grass is more plentiful along the southwestern route."

Fargo nodded. "Grass is generally plentiful after early May, but it'll start to thin out in west Texas."

"And there is the matter of terrain. My informant insists there are no major difficulties with mountain ranges. Doesn't that make this route faster?"

Fargo bit back his first reply. He knew all about these helpful "informants." Often they owned business interests along the routes they enthusiastically recommended.

"At most," Fargo said, "you might save a few weeks. And it's true there are some settlements along this route, places like San Antonio and Las Cruces, and a few good stores and trading posts. But it's mostly a better *military* route. You spent many years in northern Mexico, don Hernando. You must know about the tribes of the Southwest, especially the Kiowas, Comanches, and Apaches."

"Bad medicine," Booger threw in. "And you got the Mex'can freebooters, Comancheros—"

"Bottle it, Booger," Fargo cut him off, nodding discreetly toward the ladies.

"Yes," Quintana replied, "I am aware of those dangers, certainly. And on the subject of such dangers, I owe you the truth about the attempt on your lives a few minutes ago. It was not my men who fired on you, Senor Fargo—I strongly

27

suspect it was the work of a notorious and vicious gang out of northern Mexico. They are freebooters and *contrabandistas*, and at times form a scalper army. They also purchase slaves from the Comancheros and sell them in Chihuahua Province."

The viceroy paused and studied Fargo's face closely before adding, "They are led by a hellish monster known as El Lobo Flaco."

Fargo started visibly.

"Ah, I see by your reaction that you know who I mean?"

"I know him, all right," Fargo replied grimly. "El Lobo Flaco—the Skinny Wolf. He came within an ace of dousing my glims south of the Pecos Stream in west Texas. He's trouble raised to the fifth power. So are those lunatic hyenas who side him. If *that* bunch is in the mix, it's gonna be a rough piece of work to whip this party through to California."

The viceroy smiled. "That is why I sent for you. Rough work is your specialty, true?"

"It is," Fargo agreed on a sigh. "But I'm damned if I enjoy it. How do you know the Skinny Wolf was behind the ambush tonight?"

The viceroy's smile melted like a snowflake on a river. "He is obsessed, I believe the word is, with my daughter. Her portrait was painted by the celebrated Mexican artist Juan Gabriel Marquez and reproduced, by copperplate, all over Mexico. It was impossible to keep the news of my California expedition secret—not from his all-prying ears. He intends to abduct her for the obvious reason, and I do not mean ransom."

Fargo glanced at the young beauty, whose flashing eyes boldly met his gaze. *Damn, but she's a looker,* he thought.

"I can understand all that," he said. "But this attack on me and Booger tonight isn't all. I was dang near killed in a poison pitfall trap earlier today. How would the Skinny Wolf know I was coming to Powder-horn?"

Quintana's face twisted into an indrawn, bitter mask. "Because, my friend, I fear there is a traitor among us."

"Any idea who it is?"

Quintana stuck a pinch of snuff under his lip. "No, and it is only a suspicion."

"Could it be Captain Salazar or one of the two soldiers who seem to be joined at his hip?"

Quintana's lips twitched into a smile. "Salazar, no. Impossible. I can sympathize with your tone of voice. He is an extremely proud man—to the point of arrogance. You see, he is a graduate of Seville's elite Colegio Militario and a former *comandante* of the royal barracks in Spain's capital. As for Lieutenant Aragon and Sergeant Rivera . . . it seems unlikely they could intrigue with El Lobo Flaco without Diego knowing about it."

"Well, then," Fargo said, "if you're right, it would be one of the other men. Is it true, don Hernando, that they are former plantation workers and not soldiers?"

"True . . . and not true. You see, they were the sons of enlisted soldiers in my garrison during my viceroyalty in Mexico. They and their families escaped with me to New Orleans, where I purchased a sugarcane plantation outside the city in Faubourg Marigny. We Spaniards have outlawed slavery, and even though Louisiana law permits it, I chose to use my former soldiers, and eventually their grown children, as wage laborers."

Quintana looked pensive for a moment. "Now, unfortunately, my health forces me to the more temperate climate of Alta California, and they have elected to accompany me."

Fargo nodded. "But I've been around soldiers much of my life, and these men of yours seem to have a . . . hair-trigger readiness about them you don't find in common laborers."

"Tienes razon," Quintana replied. "You are right. That is Diego's doing. You see, he, Aragon, and Rivera were sent to protect me and Miranda after the Mexican government sent agents to make attempts on our lives. Those three have turned the rest into a well-trained citizens' militia of sorts."

Fargo caught Booger's eye for a moment, then said, "That might prove handy if the Skinny Wolf and his jackals are on your spoor. We'll also be crossing the ranges of the Kiowas and Comanches, no boys to trifle with. Both tribes have made common cause, and they've killed more whites than any other tribe. And once we get into New Mexico Territory, we might have to lock horns with Apaches."

"As to that . . . excuse me a moment, gentlemen."

Hernando Quintana stepped through the fly of the tent. Immediately his "demure" daughter spoke up.

"I saw you staring at me earlier, Mr. Fargo."

"Of course. What man with sap in him wouldn't? And you stared back."

"Certainly. You are a dashing figure of a man. Do you like what you see when you look at me?"

"Well, the ribbon is sure pretty. But what's in the package?"

Booger snickered. Katrina Robles, the duenna, spoke up. "It is time that we retire, Miranda. We will set out early, and we have many long, hard days ahead of us."

"Perhaps," Miranda suggested, coyly working her fan and watching Fargo from those bewitching eyes, "they can be made more pleasant."

"Fargo," Booger muttered with animosity, "why must *you* always be the lone rooster in the henhouse?"

Before Fargo could reply to Miranda, the viceroy stepped back inside. "If you gentlemen will kindly come outside, I have asked Ernesto to bring one of the wagons around."

Fargo wasn't all that eager to play clay pigeon again in the glaring torchlight, but he complied. A reinforced wagon sat just outside the tent.

"I am aware of the increased danger from savages along this southwestern route," Quintana explained. "So I came prepared. Ernesto, *hazlo, por favor.*"

The young *bracero* turned militiaman whisked away a canvas tarp.

"God's trousers!" Booger exclaimed. "*That's* medicine!"

"They are securely bolted to the wagon bed," Quintana said. "And there are plenty of rounds for both weapons."

Fargo took in the muzzle-loading artillery rifle and a solid brass one-pounder cannon.

"The cannon fires exploding balls," Quintana explained. "It is my understanding that the savages of the Southwest have little experience with such weapons and will likely find them very intimidating."

"Yeah, the big-thundering guns will definitely scare hell out of Kiowas and Comanches," Fargo allowed. "Not so much the Apaches, though. They've been facing Mexican armies for a long time, and they've got used to them. There's another problem, too."

"That being . . . ?"

"All three tribes prefer the sneak attack at night. Unlike the northern tribes, they got no taboo about fighting after dark. It's good to have these guns, but you best keep those men of yours vigilant all night long."

"Good advice," Quintana agreed. "I gladly defer to your experience in such matters."

Quintana loosed a long, fluming sigh. "I envy you, Skye Fargo. They say wisdom comes with age. I, for one, would rather be a bit younger and a bit more stupid."

Fargo chuckled, admiring the viceroy's candor.

"Well, gentlemen, we must start early. I apologize sincerely for making no special sleeping arrangements for you."

"Hell," Booger said, "I could sleep in a hammock filled with cats. And Fargo will not abide any walls or roof when he sleeps."

The two men said good night and headed back toward the makeshift corral to spread their blankets.

"I don't like this deal, Catfish," Booger complained.

"Something ain't quite jake," Fargo agreed. "I knew the pay was too good."

"But, say! That Miranda is a fine-haired, sweet-lavender bit of frippit, uh? I'd eat her pussy till her head caved in. And of course *you*, lucky bastard, will make the naked pretzel with her. They all lip salt from your hand."

"Never mind that. Your tongue is swinging way too loose, old campaigner. No more cracks about how heavy that coach is. Like you said, there's something queer about this deal. And in case you haven't noticed, we're not exactly surrounded by friends."

5

Five miles south of Powder-horn, Texas, stood a deserted, dilapidated wooden structure that had once been a U.S. Army mirror-relay station before the magnetic telegraph finally worked its way west of the Missouri River. Lately it had become the temporary quarters for El Lobo Flaco and his notorious gang.

"Jefe," reported the Mexican named Ramon Velasquez, "we were not able to get close enough. Fargo and the *hombre grande* with him were pinned down but not hit."

"Que suerte tan malo!" the Skinny Wolf swore quietly. "The Devil's own luck! In one day this gringo legend has eluded death twice. He is a hard man to kill, Ramon. But the cat sits by the gopher hole, *verdad*? I am a patient man, and Fargo has a long journey before him. Here, cut the dust, amigo."

El Lobo sat at a crumbling deal table drinking from a bottle of the milky cactus liquor known as pulque. He handed the bottle to his *segundo*. El Lobo was a thin but sinewy man with a skullish, tight-to-the-bone face and a lipless grin. He wore leather *chivarra* pants with a silver concho belt, a rawhide vest, and a low-crowned black hat that left most of his face in sinister shadow in the flickering light on an old skunk-oil lamp.

"Where are the rest of the men?" Velasquez asked after drinking pulque and wiping his mouth on the back of his hand.

The Skinny Wolf flashed a mouthful of tobacco-stained teeth. "Where else? Out back taking turns on the *indio* girl we brought back from the raid on Poca Agua. It is a good thing the two of us bulled her first, for I assure you she is no longer as tight as a mouse's ear. They have not let up on her."

Even as he fell silent, a piercing cry rent the fabric of the night. Ramon's smallpox-scarred face divided itself in a smile.

"Paco must be doing some knife work on her, uh, *jefe*?"

El Lobo flashed his lipless grin. "Yes. It would seem that we are rough unshaven men with poor manners. But once we capture Hernando Quintana's coach, no one will care about our manners. That will not come to pass, however, until we have put this Trailsman below the horizon."

"According to our spy, they still have about eighteen *soldados*," Velasquez reminded his boss. "Well-armed soldiers."

"Only three who are true soldiers and battle tested, Ramon, and of course one of those three we do not need to worry about. As for the others—yes, they can march and drill and lick the fingers of their masters. And Miguel claims they can fight. But all of us have survived shooting battles—with the *famoso* Rangers of Texas, with the godless Apaches, with the Guardia Civil of our own nation. No, the only rock we will split on is Fargo—the 'savage angel' as he is called in the fawning *norteamericano* newspapers."

"Thanks to these same newspapers," Velasquez pointed out, "Fargo's death could prove quite profitable. His severed head could be packed in brine, like a buffalo tongue, and put on display for a *precio* of a few centavos."

Another almost inhuman scream from behind the old station was followed by raucous, drunken laughter and cheers.

"This foolish viceroy," Velasquez said. "Do you believe his secret plan can work?"

The Skinny Wolf nodded. "Not with the small number of men with him now. But Miguel claims that hundreds more are waiting in Alta California. *Vaya!* Two men who drink black coffee could take that unprotected state—but, of course, it will never come to that. Not after we seize that coach."

El Lobo wore a .41-caliber magazine pistol in a canvas holster under his left armpit. He pulled it out and laid it on the table.

"Tell Paco to put his knife away and bring the girl in," he told Velasquez. "I have thought of a plan for her."

Velasquez stepped outside under a vast night sky peppered silver with stars. He shouted an order, and a moment later a drunken man appeared in the doorway.

"Con permiso, jefe?"

"Pase."

Paco half led, half dragged a slender young Papago Indian girl inside. She had been stripped naked, and several knife slashes on her arms and legs streamed blood. Her dark eyes were glassy with shock, her face and badly scraped and bruised body smudged with dirt.

A close look, however, revealed that she had once been a beautiful girl before this bunch of devils unleashed from hell descended on her small, peaceful farming village south of Matamoros, Mexico.

"Oye, chica," the Skinny Wolf said, picking up his pistol. "Listen, girl, I know you speak my language. Would you like me to shoot you?"

She nodded, her eyes begging him to do it.

The Skinny Wolf laughed. "I will. But first I wish to show you something. Ramon, bring the *morral.*"

Velasquez reached into a corner. He grabbed a bulging fiber bag and set it on the table. El Lobo spilled its contents out—a heap of bloody scalps. The girl retched and her knees buckled, but Paco held her up.

"The *gobernador* of Chihuahua," El Lobo taunted her, "has declared war on the Apaches. He pays a generous bounty for each scalp. But, of course, many *indios* in Mexico have the same coarse black hair as Apaches. And Apaches are very difficult to kill—unlike you dirt scratchers who have been Christianized by the Spanish padres. All your prayers to a virgin who had a child without spreading her legs for a man, and *look* what it got you, *estupida.*"

"The *gauchupines,*" she said, using a Southwest Indian term of contempt for Spaniards. "They drove us in herds like cows to their churches to warn us about the Devil. But you Mexicans are the true devils!"

El Lobo laughed with delight. "Yes, straight from hell. And I am the leader of all the devils."

He used the muzzle of his pistol to pull out one silver scalp that still had a tortoiseshell comb in it.

"Do you recognize this, *estupida*?"

The girl's dirty and bruised face twisted into a mask of

sheer horror and revulsion. "*Abuela*," she managed, choking back a sob.

"Yes, your grandmother. A dried-up old crone who will earn me one hundred pesos. And this pile has the hair of the rest of your family and of all in your village. Only one is missing . . . Paco!"

The girl was too weak and spirit broken to resist when the brutish Mexican threw her to the rammed-earth floor and drew the bone-handle knife from his sash. Placing one knee on her neck, he made a swift, savage outline cut. Then he entwined his fingers in her long hair and gave a mighty jerk. The scalp snapped loose with a sound like hundreds of tiny bubbles popping.

Her piteous shriek of pain was cut short when the Skinny Wolf's pistol bucked in his fist. Her bladder emptied reflexively in death, and the stench of urine, blood, and spent powder stained the air.

"Drag her outside, Paco," El Lobo ordered his minion. "We will use her to send in our calling card to Fargo. This time, unlike out at the Pecos River, the *famoso* gringo in buckskins will not outwit me. *Lo juro*—I swear it!"

Even before the birds began celebrating sunup, Fargo and Booger were tying in to a piping-hot breakfast of buckwheat cakes, soda biscuits, and ham gravy.

The three Spanish soldiers and Hernando Quintana's former plantation workers had taken their food and separated themselves in a group well away from the *norteamericanos*. But don Hernando and the two young women, in a gesture of civility, remained near the cooking fire with Fargo, Booger, Bitch Creek McDade, the wrangler, and the cook, Deke Lafferty.

Deke goggled at Booger as the huge reinsman devoured an entire buckwheat cake in one mouthful. "Holy Hannah, Booger! Can you eat just *one* cow?"

Booger belched so loudly that Miranda Quintana and Katrina Robles winced.

"Yes, if we are forced to half rations," Booger replied.

Fargo glanced toward the group of Spaniards. Yesterday

only the three uniformed soldiers had openly carried weapons. But now every former "plantation worker" was armed with a rifle and a Colt Navy revolver, and many wore crossed bandoliers stuffed with rounds.

"I am told, Senor Fargo," the viceroy remarked, "that the route we are taking is quite familiar to you."

Fargo nodded, blowing on his coffee. The well-established southern route to California crossed all of Texas, a good chunk of New Mexico Territory, a corner of Utah, and then up coastal California. The next major stop was San Antonio, and from there along the San Antonio Road to El Paso. From there it was on to Fort Yuma where they would ford the Colorado River. Major settlements and resupply points along the way included Las Cruces and, much nearer, Victoria, Texas.

"It's been pretty well traveled since the army finished it in 1849," Fargo replied, "but mostly by troops and mail carriers or well-protected bull trains. Mainly that's because Powderhorn is hard to reach by land from the north."

"Yes, but steamers arrive five times a week from New Orleans, the principal reason I settled on this route. I am told the road is well tracked and defined."

Again Fargo nodded. "The first two hundred and fifty miles are well settled, and supplies can be had at reasonable rates. But you don't seem to lack for supplies."

While this conversation went forward, both of the women had been watching Fargo with great interest—a fact, Fargo noticed, that had not escaped a sullen Captain Diego Salazar. The women sat in camp chairs sipping from porcelain mugs of coffee.

Booger winked at Fargo, then addressed himself to the ladies. "Now, girls, old Booger feels it's his duty to warn you—when you're out west, *never* drink to the bottom of your cup or glass."

"But why?" Miranda asked.

"Well, like as not, you'll find some little critter there. Why, I knew a feller in west Texas who drained a cup of coffee. The poor fool swallowed thousands of chigger eggs that was mixed with the dregs."

"Did he become ill?" Katrina Robles asked.

"Ill? Why, sugarplum, them eggs hatched in his innards, and he got et to death from the inside out."

There was enough light for Fargo to watch both women pale. Hernando Quintana concealed a smile behind his hand.

"Mr. Fargo," Miranda said, "is that the truth?"

Fargo's strong white teeth flashed out of his crop-bearded, weather-tanned face. "Miss Quintana, Booger McTeague is the biggest liar since Simon Peter denied Christ. But he's got a point—I always spill out the lees myself. Many's the time I've found a surprise at the bottom of a cup."

"Then I will defer to your experience," she replied, making that last word resonate with layers of possibility.

She gave Fargo a wanton look that he immediately felt in his hip pocket.

Interesting, he thought. This Spanish-American beauty was young, all right, but a full-grown woman with a woman's knowledge in her eyes. And it wasn't just the color and lines that gave value to the best horses *or* women. It was a mysterious quality the Spanish called *brio escondido*, "the hidden vigor." And Fargo suspected this feisty filly was brimming over with it.

Diego Salazar had edged close enough to overhear this last snippet of conversation. He strolled quickly closer; his wire-tight mouth set like a trap in grim disapproval.

"Senorita Quintana," he said primly, "I beg leave respectfully to remind you that a lady of your station should not converse so freely with . . . hired labor. It is unseemly."

"Now, now, Diego," Quintana intervened, "I would hardly call a man of Fargo's reputation and accomplishments a servant."

Salazar bowed deferentially. "We are ready to embark at any time, don Hernando."

Booger, steamed at the officer's high-hatting manner, opened his mouth to hurl an insult. But Fargo dug an elbow into his ribs. "Caulk up, knothead," he muttered.

While Deke, McDade, and some of the *braceros* broke camp, Fargo checked the loads in his walnut-grip Colt, palming the wheel to make sure the action was true. The night before he had adjusted the sights on his Henry from two hundred to three hundred yards, allowing for longer-distance attacks in this open vastness of east Texas. He had also honed the blade of his big Arkansas toothpick on a whetstone, making sure the "unholy trinity"—Booger's sarcastic name for Diego Salazar and his two companions—saw him.

"Tarnal hell, Fargo," Booger complained when the two were out of earshot of the Spaniards. "Does your mother know you're out? That cockchafer Salazar is tryin' to put the shawl on you. I'm dogged and gone iffen *I* would swallow his bunk."

Booger pulled on the large pair of buckskin gauntlets that no respectable driver would be caught without.

"I take it you ain't too fond of him," Fargo said from a deadpan.

"Does asparagus make your piss stink? I would whip that toy soldier until his hair falls out."

Fargo whistled to the Ovaro and he came trotting over.

"Right now we got bigger fish to fry, old roadster. There's already been two attempts to kill us. We're smack in the middle of open country, easier to spot than bedbugs on a clean sheet. And it's gonna stay that way for a long stretch."

"Pah! How do you know that the sons a' bitches tryin' to point our toes to the sky ain't feeding at the same trough with these Espanish?"

Fargo tossed on blanket, pad, and saddle. "I don't. When's the last time you heard of a civilian expedition hauling along a cannon with exploding shells? This whole deal stinks like a whorehouse at low tide."

"Tell the truth and shame the Devil. Me and you been bamboozled, Trailsman."

"That's why I plan to say little and hear much. And you best do the same. Keep your eyes to all sides up on that box. I got a gut hunch we're up against it, Booger—up against it hard, old son, and a man never hears the shot that kills him."

Fargo had to admit, as he watched the Quintana caravan shudder into westward motion, that he was impressed by the former viceroy's planning.

The chuck wagon, fodder wagons, and other freight conveyances were of quality construction. Two entire freight wagons were reserved for extra tongues, iron tires, coupling poles, whippletrees, kingbolts, and other spare parts to cover any breakdown. The mules and horses, which McDade had tied on lead lines behind the various conveyances, were of superior quality. Booger's saddle ox lumbered along behind one of the fodder wagons.

It had not been necessary to hire any extra drivers besides Booger. Deke Lafferty handled the lines for the chuck wagon, McDade for the largest fodder wagon. The rest were driven by Quintana's former workers—and with evident skill Fargo found surprising in men who supposedly worked on a sugarcane plantation.

Once the party was fairly under way, Fargo followed his usual scouting pattern for flat, open country. Instead of riding out ahead, he circled the train in ever-expanding circles, relying often on his army binoculars with their 7X lenses. In places the blue-green saw grass grew higher than his stirrups, and the danger of ambush was constant.

So far all seemed peaceful enough. Nonetheless, Fargo felt what the mountain men called a "truth goose"—a premonitory tingle on the back of his neck. Trouble was out there somewhere, and Fargo reminded himself of the frontiersman's credo: *The readiness is all.*

During a midmorning break to spell the pulling teams, Fargo rode in to confer with Booger.

"Those wheels are cutting mighty deep," he remarked, keeping his voice low.

"That's no shit," Booger replied. "Skye, there's only Quintana and the two women inside this rig—not a one of them three is heavy. Now, old Booger is a big sumbitch, f'sure. But I got *eight* strong mules in the traces, and, mister, I mean they're puttin' their shoulders into it. Country like this? Hell, four jennies could get it did easy."

"Well, the old man is rich, after all, and he's moving lock, stock, and barrel. Would you trust to bank drafts if you had a fortune? Hell, I wouldn't leave a pair of old shoes behind in New Orleans for safekeeping let alone a heap of money."

"That's the straight," Booger agreed. "Them banks is all crooked as cat shit. But Christmas crackers! How rich can he be? I've hauled a hunnert thousand in gold bars, and it don't bog a coach like thissen is."

"Whatever the deal is," Fargo decided, "it's none of our mix—yet."

Miranda Quintana poked her beautiful face out one of the windows. "What are you two whispering about, Mr. Fargo? Naughty things?"

Fargo grinned and touched his hat. "No, Miss Quintana, but when I look at you my thoughts run in that direction."

"I was under the impression that your reputation is based on actions, not thoughts."

"Miranda!" Katrina Robles's voice scolded. "*Basta ya!* That is enough!"

Booger winked at Fargo. "Push-push, huh? Won't be long, Catfish, and you'll have her barking like a dog."

The grin bled from Booger's round, sunburned face. "Look at that greaser pig shit Rivera."

Fargo followed Booger's gaze. Sergeant Rivera, flanked by Diego Salazar and Lieutenant Juan Aragon, had dismounted nearby to smoke. Rivera, staring pointedly at the two newest arrivals, pulled his machete from its shoulder scabbard and polished the blade on his trouser leg.

"The bigger the blade, the smaller the man," Booger muttered. "*That* one's wearing the no-good label."

Rivera called out, "*Oye, gordo!* Listen, fat man! When is the last time you saw your own feet?"

"I can't miss 'em, Sancho, thanks to these Spanish moccasins! See wherever I go, dago!"

"Clean your ears or cut your hair," Fargo warned Booger. "I said don't agitate this bunch, savvy!"

"Fargo," Booger exploded, "fuck you *and* the horse you rode in on! I'll be goddamn if I'm lettin' these—"

"Senor McTeague," Hernando Quintana complained from inside the coach, "you have every right to defend yourself from my ill-mannered men. But please monitor your language when ladies can hear you."

"Sorry," Booger called back, his tone surly. He shot Fargo a homicidal glower and then snapped the lines. "Gerlong there, mules! G'long! *Whoop!*"

Stifling a grin, Fargo decided to gig the Ovaro forward for a quick squint out front. He generally preferred open country, but the scant tree cover made skylining a real danger on horseback in this saw grass. He loosened the Henry in its boot and kept his eyes on the prowl, watching for motion and reflections, not shapes.

Something well ahead of him on the narrow road prompted Fargo to break out his field glass. He raised them, focused, focused them finer, and got his first good luck.

A crooked stove-lid hat.

Fargo swore without heat.

"It *can't* be," he muttered, the remark more like a prayer than a statement.

But even as he thumped the Ovaro up to a canter, he knew exactly who it was.

"Wait until Captain Christ Almighty Salazar sees *this*," he told the Ovaro. "Old warhorse, this is definitely gonna cap the climax."

6

The two Indians squatted patiently beside the trail, watching Fargo approach. The older, a Shawnee who for some mysterious reason called himself Cherokee Bob, watched Fargo from eyes like black agates. His companion was a fat-assed Delaware called All Behind Him. It was his crooked, bright red stove-lid hat that Fargo had recognized.

Fargo reined in. "The hell are you two grifters doing hanging around here?"

The Shawnee and Delaware tribes had been closely associated for almost two centuries and were highly nomadic even among plains warriors. He had seen men of both tribes on the Pacific shore in the West, on Hudson Bay up north, and deep into Mexico in the South. As a rule Fargo had found both tribes intelligent, brave, and reliable, eternal wanderers who were welcome even among the clannish Mormons of Utah.

But then again, there were exceptions to every rule, and Fargo was looking at two of them now.

"Fargo," Cherokee Bob said solemnly in halting English, "you have taste the waters of Manitu, and Indian legend say it will always call you back, for you are—"

Fargo cut him off. "Never mind that horse shit. Knock off the baby talk, too. What's your grift this time?"

Cherokee Bob snickered and waved a hand as if shooing off a fly. Fargo winced when the Shawnee turned his head to spit: half his left ear was missing, chewed off by a Crow warrior during a pony raid up north near the Black Hills.

"Ah, hell, I never could honeyfuggle you, Fargo," he admitted in perfectly pronounced English. "We heard about this Spanish expedition to California, figured to travel along and fleece these sons of Coronado. Ain't like these turds haven't porked the red man plenty."

"Fleece 'em? The way these hotheaded dons feel about Indians? Hell, you'll be lucky if they don't flay your soles and turn your skulls into chamber pots."

Cherokee Bob's piercing black eyes met Fargo's pure blue ones. "Think?"

After a few seconds it was Fargo's turn to grin. "Nah. You two scoundrels could rook a nun out of her virtue. I'd *ought* to feel sorry for 'em, but I'd chuck the whole lot for a ginger snap."

So far, All Behind Him, more taciturn than his companion, had said nothing. Fargo watched him scratch at the beggar lice leaping off his clothing.

"Where's your horses?" Fargo asked him.

"Ate 'em," the Delaware replied. His eyes suddenly filmed with tears.

"He liked his horse," Cherokee Bob explained.

"It's sad to lose a good horse," Fargo sympathized.

"No," the Shawnee clarified. "I mean he *liked* it. We jerked the meat and it was delicious. Finally ran out yesterday. He's been weeping ever since. He blubbers when he's hungry."

Fargo shook his head. "The Noble Red Man," he said sarcastically. "You two need to get friendly with a bit of Castile soap. You stink like a jakes."

He rummaged in a saddle pocket, then flipped a sack of stale corn dodgers down to them. "Best I can do for you right now."

Both Indians tore into the food like hungry bears ripping into a honeycomb.

"How's the eats with this Spanish bunch?" Cherokee Bob demanded around a mouthful of food.

"Aces high," Fargo told him. "They got a fine cook. His biscuits are so light you have to hold them down."

"Here come the *conquistadors* now," Bob said sarcastically.

Fargo slewed around in the saddle. Salazar, Aragon, and Rivera were galloping their horses toward them, faces grim and belligerent.

"Best watch this bunch," Fargo warned. "Especially the pig-eyed one with the machete."

The two Indians continued to devour corn dodgers, apparently unconcerned.

"Fargo," Salazar demanded as he reined in, "why haven't you killed these two savages?"

"Why would I?" Fargo replied. "They haven't tried to kill me."

"Yes, I have heard that you are an Indian lover."

"He sure is, Captain." Cherokee Bob spoke up. "He's loved plenty of them right onto their funeral scaffolds."

"He speaks English?" Lieutenant Aragon demanded.

Fargo nodded. "And Spanish, and French and maybe a dozen Indian tongues."

"I can palaver a little Russian, too," Cherokee Bob boasted.

"You *know* him?" Salazar asked Fargo, incredulous.

"Well, we ain't exactly swapping spit," Fargo said. "And I wouldn't leave my horse with either one of them. But these two have done some good work for the U.S. Army. That's how I met them."

Rivera spat into the road inches from Cherokee Bob's feet. "*Mira, Capitan!* Look at their eyes! Four pieces of glass in a whore's brass ring. If they possess souls, then I am the sultan of Persia."

"Ease off," Fargo warned him. "These two are more dangerous than they look."

"They are vermin. Godless heathens. And can you not smell them? Vermin must be exterminated."

Fargo knew what was coming.

"Crick," Cherokee Bob said softly to his companion.

"Crack," All Behind Him responded.

Rivera's machete was only halfway out of its scabbard when the two "vermin" made their move. All Behind Him reached into the moth-eaten blanket in his lap and produced a Manhattan Arms pepperbox pistol. All six barrels were capped, primed, and loaded.

However, it was the weapon Cherokee Bob produced from behind his ratty corduroy jacket that made all three Spaniards goggle and Fargo grin.

"Cristo!" Rivera swore, his blunt face paling.

The antique but lethal weapon now aimed at Rivera's belly was a literal "hand cannon"—a miniature cast-iron cannon that fired a two-ounce ball capable of dropping an elephant dead in its tracks. The barrel was mounted on a heavy wooden pistol grip, and the original fuse hole was now covered by a spring-activated flintlock mechanism.

"Innit a little honey?" Cherokee Bob said proudly. "I once blew a shit house to smithereens with it in St. Louis."

Fargo added, "Those hand cannons are heavy and not too accurate past thirty yards. But they'll blow a hole the size of South Pass through a man. They'd have to bury you with a rake, Rivera."

Rivera left his machete sheathed. "Do not point it at me like that, you ignorant, gut-eating savage."

Salazar turned his cruelly handsome face toward Fargo. "I was told that Texas law does not permit Negroes or Indians to own firearms."

"You take it from him," Fargo suggested.

Booger, noticing that a game was afoot ahead of him, had laid in to his buckskin whip. By this time Hernando Quintana's fine coach had rolled to a stop beside the group.

"Ha-ho, ha-ho!" Booger exclaimed, sizing up the situation and liking it just fine. *"Fire* that smoke wagon, Injin! That garlic needs killing."

"Senor Fargo," Quintana called out the window, so nervous he forgot to speak in English, *"que tenemos aqui?"*

"What we have here," Fargo replied, "are a Shawnee and a Delaware Indian. Most of them live along the Missouri and Canadian rivers, and I'd rate both tribes some of the best hunters, trackers, and scouts in the West. The army swears by them."

"We'd like to string along with you folks," Cherokee Bob added. "Just to work for our eats. We wouldn't live in your camp, of course—just trail along."

Quintana studied both of them, his face polite but dubious. "But we don't need hunters, and Fargo is our guide."

"They possess other skills," Fargo said without elaborating.

Quintana looked at the Indians again, then at Fargo. "The decision is yours. Could they be of any use?"

Fargo debated that. They could certainly be useful if they chose to. Cherokee Bob knew most of the Kiowa and Comanche renegade battle chiefs in the Southwest, and he was an excellent negotiator at arranging "private treaties" with them.

On the other hand, both of these itinerant grifters would steal a steamboat and come back for the river. Both of them were trickier than a redheaded woman and far better at running a flimflam than at making themselves useful.

"Don Hernando, bethink yourself." Captain Salazar interceded. "Surely you jest? *Por Dios!* These are godless savages armed with dangerous weapons."

That tore it for Fargo. He enjoyed the hell out of watching the pompous graduate of "Seville's elite Colegio Militario" stew in his juices.

"I think you should take them on," Fargo told his employer. "We've got some rough Indian ranges ahead of us, and these two could prove useful. And they'd make good roving sentries on our perimeter at night."

"So be it," the viceroy replied. "I trust your judgment in these matters. But please make sure they boil their clothing and bathe."

Salazar again started to object, but Quintana waved him quiet. "The matter is settled, Diego."

Booger, watching his archnemesis, Sergeant Rivera, turn apoplectic with rage, grinned like the cat who fucked the canary before he ate it. He was about to crack his whip when Cherokee Bob spoke up.

"Hold your horses a moment, big fellow. I was noticing your moccasins. I'll bet you five dollars I can tell you right where you got them."

Booger, who loved a wager, looked at him asquint. "That's money for old rope, John. But have you *got* five dollars? That's heap big wampum for a blanket ass."

Cherokee Bob looked at Fargo, who had to bite his lip hard to keep a straight face. "I'll cover his end of the bet, Booger."

"I'll sweeten the bet," Cherokee Bob added. "If I can't tell you *exactly* where you got them moccasins, I'll pay you five dollars. If you lose, you only gotta pony up a dollar."

"Money in the bank," Booger scoffed. "Ain't no way in hell you could know where I got 'em. Even Fargo don't know that. You're on, featherhead."

"You got them *on your feet*."

Booger purpled with rage while Cherokee Bob shook with the silent "abdomen laugh" Indians had perfected for treaty signings.

"Heathen, you can kiss my—"

"Pay up," Fargo snapped. "No need to get your back up— you walked right into it."

"H'ar, now! He—"

"I will not abide any man who welches on a bet. *I* paid up when he burned me with it at Fort Smith."

Booger dug a silver dollar from a chamois pouch on his belt and threw it down beside the trail. "Fargo, you double-poxed hound, I—"

"We're waiting, Mr. McTeague," Quintana called out his window.

"I suggest you folks wait a little longer." Cherokee Bob spoke up. "And make sure those women stay put."

He looked at Fargo, the mirth fading from his face. "There's something up ahead you need to see. And I'll warn you right now—it ain't too pretty."

Fargo reined in and swung down from the saddle. He had seen plenty of brutality in his day, and on occasion he had been responsible for some. But what he stared at now taxed him to the limits of his endurance.

The naked girl who lay—or, rather, lay heaped—across the trail was barely recognizable as human. Her severed head—minus the scalp—and limbs had been tossed on top of her entrails. A squirming, shifting blue-black blanket of flies buzzed so loudly the horses nervously stutter-stepped away.

"Is she a Mexican?" Salazar asked, averting his eyes. Lieutenant Aragon hastily retreated and retched into the grass. But Sergeant Rivera, Fargo noticed, just seemed bored as he gazed stone-eyed at the unspeakable atrocity.

"Could be a *mestizo*," Fargo replied, meaning of mixed Mexican and Indian blood. "Or most likely a full-blooded Indian. Her cheekbones are high and pronounced."

"What does it matter now?" Rivera asked. He swiped irritably at the flies.

"*Las moscas* are eating her as we speak. The ancient Christian rite of human sacrifice is a purification ritual that binds the holy. Binds them as one against the infidels and pagans who obstruct God's perfect plan."

Fargo fought off a sudden impulse to kill the smug bastard on the spot. "Pagans like me, you mean?"

"Sergeant Rivera was not condoning this barbarism," Salazar said. "It was merely a philosophical observation."

Booger and the two Indians had followed on foot. They arrived now.

"I see the butcher's bill was steep," Booger said, removing his hat and swiping at the flies. "This is a rough piece of work even for Comanches."

Fargo shook his head. "Don't put it on them. Comanches are like Apaches. They got little use for scalps. Somebody else did it."

He looked at the Shawnee and the Delaware. "Did you see who did it?"

"See it?" Lieutenant Aragon repeated. "Perhaps they did it."

"Didn't see her killed," Cherokee Bob said, ignoring Aragon. "But me and All Behind Him was hiding in the grass when a Mexican dumped her. Had her rolled up in a ground sheet. I ain't certain, but it looked like one of them shithouse rats who ride with El Lobo Flaco."

Fargo nodded. "That's how I make it, too. They sell scalps down in Mexico. She was dumped so we'd find her. Especially so I'd find her."

Fargo looked at Salazar. "Here's what I don't savvy. Your boss claims the Skinny Wolf has taken a freak to abduct Miranda. I can believe that easy enough. But this ain't the best way to win a gal's heart. You sure he's not after something else?"

Salazar's eyes narrowed to slits and his nostrils flared. "You are calling His Excellency a liar?"

"T'hell with that 'His Excellency' hogwash, Sancho," Booger cut in. "He ain't no damn king nor prince. He's a man what pulls his pants down to shit like everybody else.

'Cept for Rivera here—when he needs to shit he just takes off his hat."

Booger's imposing stature and the fierce warning in his eyes startled all three Spaniards. He was still outraged about being fleeced for a dollar and looking to vent his fury on somebody. Salazar finally spoke up, but in a muted tone.

"*Norteamericanos* like you two place no great importance on lineage. In Spain, a man is the sum total of his bloodline. Many men in America cannot even name their great-grandfathers. I can name my sires and dams back to the time of the Moors. You two are certainly capable men, and no doubt fearless. But like most men in this godforsaken frontier, you are rootless. Thus you have no respect for subordination—every man knowing and accepting his place in the social order."

"My *root* is plenty long," Booger punned. "Sires and dams? Pah! My great-grandfather never bought me a whiskey, so piss on him."

"Ease off, Booger," Fargo said. "The man wasn't insulting us, just making a point. Anyhow, we got bigger problems to fret. The Skinny Wolf and his pack can't be that far away."

"The pig's afterbirth who dumped this body," Booger said, "had to leave a trail in this grass."

Fargo nodded. "And we could waste time following it. But I know El Lobo and his ways. He won't roost long in one place, especially after something like this. And he's a top hand at luring men into ambushes. Our best chance to kill him is when he comes to us—and he will, sure as cats fighting."

Again he looked at Salazar, his eyes as direct and piercing as bullets. "Hernando Quintana strikes me as a wise man who doesn't jump to conclusions. And he told me he thinks El Lobo has a man traveling with this party."

"If you are implying, Fargo, that I—"

"Come down off your hind legs, Captain. It's obvious you're smitten by his daughter, so why would you want to help a filthy scum bucket like El Lobo lay hands on her?"

"Fargo," Booger cut in, "you yourself said the Skinny Wolf could be after something besides the girl."

49

Fargo spoke up quickly before Booger mentioned the much-too-heavy coach.

"Yeah, but even if he is, you think he wouldn't grab her? He's notorious for stealing beautiful women. Salazar, I'm just asking if you've got any suspicions about anybody in this expedition."

"I respect don Hernando immensely, but he may be wrong. These men are all loyal to His Excellency and to Spain."

To Spain. Fargo found that remark a mite queer, but predictably, Booger had to stir up more trouble.

"I say it's this shifty-eyed bastard Rivera," he announced. "He looks like the type who would kill a nun for her gold tooth and then sell her bones to a rendering plant."

Rivera's blunt, brutish face darkened with rage, but before he could react Booger, moving swiftly for such a big man and roaring like a burned bear, picked him up and flung him fifteen feet out into the grass like a sack of tripes.

Cherokee Bob and All Behind Him howled with mirth. Salazar and Aragon looked shell-shocked at this astounding show of strength—Rivera was hardly a small man.

"Booger," Fargo said wearily, "take one of these red aboriginals back with you. You stay behind with the coach and make sure nobody else comes forward. Send a shovel back so I can bury these remains."

Rivera struggled to his feet with his Volcanic repeater at the level. In an eyeblink Fargo jerked back his six-shooter and blew the weapon out of Rivera's hand.

"Booger, get a damn wiggle on," Fargo snapped. "He needs time to cool down."

"Aye, he'll be *cool*, Catfish," Booger said as he grabbed Cherokee Bob by the collar and headed out, "when old Booger rips out his liver and feeds it to his asshole."

All Behind Him, still digging at lice, finally spoke up. "Fargo? When we eat?"

Fargo shook his head in disgust. El Lobo Flaco, the most dangerous killer in northern Mexico and the American Southwest, had drawn a bead on the Quintana party; Booger was on the verge of starting a war with Spain; Rivera was likely to shoot both Americans in the back; and to top it off,

Hernando Quintana appeared to be lying through his teeth about something mighty consequential.

Again Salazar's odd remark picked at Fargo like a burr in his boot: *"These men are all loyal to His Excellency and to Spain."*

Fargo gazed south across the flat, unending sea of waving saw grass. Soon the Gulf Coast would be behind them and the Texas brushland—an ambusher's paradise—would begin. The Skinny Wolf and his jackals wouldn't waste that opportunity, and here was a shifty-eyed Delaware Indian demanding to know when he could get outside some hot grub.

"I *knew* the money was too good," Fargo muttered, keeping a close eye on Rivera.

On the other hand, there were two very tempting women among this party, and both of them had been giving Fargo looks he recognized well. But that pleasant thought faded like a retinal afterimage when Fargo glanced at the butchered corpse heaped on the trail.

7

For the next week the Quintana party made excellent progress across the southeast Texas flatland. The tall saw grass quickly gave way to short-grass plains. Unlike the overgrazed Oregon Trail, the grass remained plentiful, as did good water.

But near the end of that first week, the terrain along the Southwest Trail began to change noticeably. Grass was still available, but now they encountered stretches of starved bushes, sage, and greasewood, interspersed with thick stands of thorny brush. The sun beat down with furnace heat by late afternoon, and at times water was scarce.

They were entering the deceptively dangerous Texas brushland, and now Fargo doubled his vigilance. Foremost in his mind was El Lobo Flaco, the Skinny Wolf, and the cutthroat berserkers who rode with him. The expedition was also edging into ranges familiar to Kiowas and Comanches, two tribes that had made common cause and killed more white men than any other tribes on the frontier.

However, Fargo knew from rueful experience that not all the threats were human.

Texas, in 1861, was home to millions of wild longhorns vastly different in temperament from the domesticated breeds of cattle common in Europe and England. Unlike the more placid shorthorns and white-face Herefords, these wild longhorns had arrived with the Spanish explorers centuries ago and were the first breed of cattle to freely range North America.

Wily and extremely deadly, some were man killers—literal bovine assassins—that hid in natural coverts and attacked humans. Four-legged bushwhackers adding to the danger from the two-legged breed.

Ladinos, Mexicans called them—"the sly ones." Twice Fargo had been attacked by them in the past, and both times he escaped hard death by a hairbreadth.

"Skye Fargo, surely you are exaggerating?" teased a skeptical Miranda Quintana. "Homicidal cows? Is this another Western 'yarn' such as Mr. McTeague's tale about creatures at the bottom of the glass that eat men from the inside out?"

The sun was sinking in a scarlet blaze, and Fargo had called everyone for a meeting just before supper to emphasize the various dangers of the brushland.

"Fargo ain't joshing, miss," Deke Lafferty chimed in as he knelt over one of his Dutch ovens. "I crossed Texas once slinging hash for a crew of freighters. One a' them sons of—uh, them *ladinos* attacked us at breakfast. We was mighty lucky one of the drivers had him a Hawken rifle. Them wild cows is hard to bring down when the charge is on."

Diego Salazar was smoking a thin black cigar and keeping a close eye on Miranda—something he did religiously when the regal beauty was anywhere near Fargo.

"*Oye, compadres*," he said to Aragon and Rivera, "*este hombre Fargo tiene miedo de las vacas! Que valor, eh?*"

"He did not say he feared cows, Diego." Viceroy Quintana censured his man. "He is simply warning us of danger. We would all be wise to heed him."

Booger had whipped Overland stages across Texas and knew Fargo was telling the truth. But his contrary nature made him address himself to Miranda.

"Cupcake, Skye Fargo is a notorious liar, coward, and reprobate, and you were right to call him on it. He would steal the coppers from a dead man's eyes and then rob the widow's house while she was at the funeral. Why, he—"

"My name is *not* 'cupcake,'" she said archly, "and your buffoonery is both vulgar and boring."

Booger glanced at Fargo and shrugged his massive shoulders. "Crikes! Ain't *she* death to the Devil? Maybe somebody stole her rattle when she was a baby."

"Bottle it," Fargo snapped.

Sergeant Rivera's malevolence toward the giant reinsman had increased tenfold since Booger tossed him through the air like a child's ball.

"Tonto," he spat at Booger, scorn poison-tipping the word.

Deke spoke up before Booger could. "Fargo, I wish you'd get them damn featherheads in line. I got food disappearing, and I'm missing a bottle of our medicine whiskey."

Even as he finished his complaint, Cherokee Bob's drunken voice—off-key and rusty—reached them out of the gathering darkness.

> *Buffalo gal, won't cha*
> *come out tonight,*
> *come out tonight,*
> *come out tonight . . .*

"Yeah, I'll talk to them," Fargo said, knowing it wouldn't do a damn bit of good. "But they've been useful to us. They make good picket guards at night, and I've got them watching for sign."

"Perhaps," Salazar suggested sarcastically, "they could bell these wild cows?"

"Maybe," Fargo said mildly, letting it go. He was more interested in the sultry glances being sent his way by Miranda—and in a less obvious way, by Katrina Robles, the woman supposedly keeping Miranda on the straight and narrow path.

After supper, Fargo, Booger, Deke, and Bitch Creek McDade drank coffee and smoked in a circle around a crackling fire of dead juniper wood.

"Christ," Deke said, "these damn garlics are all clabber-lipped greenhorns. Not a one of that bunch believes Fargo 'bout the *ladinos*."

"I'm a bit of a greenhorn myself," McDade chipped in, "and I don't reckon that all Spaniards are cruel. But have you boys noticed how hard Salazar and his two chums use their horses? I've seen Salazar spur that fine Arabian of his in the shoulders."

Fargo nodded. Sloppy and careless treatment of horses was bad enough, but outright cruelty rated high in his bad books—and said plenty about the men who meted out such treatment.

"Salazar and that fish-eyed Aragon are double-barreled

assholes," Booger said. "But that cockchafer Rivera is of a scurvy disposition, chappies. Say, Fargo, you palaver some Espanish—that half-faced groat called me a *tonto*. The hell's that mean?"

"Couldn't tell you," Fargo lied.

Deke cussed. "Old man Quintana is a decent sort. But that Salazar and them two boyfriends of his really gripe my ass. Damn their bones to hell, anyway! They treat me and Bitch here like ignut chawbacons. The sons a' bitches dress up in them gold braids and fancy cheese knives and swagger it around like they was ten inches taller'n God. Yessir, there's them as figgers a poor man ain't no better'n a flea-bit hound."

Booger loosed an explosive belch. "It's about damn time we killed all three of them three-penny soldiers—'r at least that skunk-bit Rivera."

"Look," Fargo said, "Booger, you and Deke need to ease off. The Skinny Wolf is likely out there right now, planning his next attack. Don't waste your fighting fettle on trifles. That cunning bastard is a heap more dangerous right now than these Spanish fops."

"When you think they'll hit us, Skye?" McDade asked.

Fargo shrugged. "How long is a piece of string? I tangled with that curly wolf near the Pecos Stream, and every time I thought I had him in my sights he worked a fox play on me."

Cherokee Bob's drunken, disembodied voice reached them out of the surrounding darkness, his singing wretched: "She has freckles on her, b-u-u-t I love her. . . ."

"Them two Injins are a sin to Moses," Deke said with a chuckle in his voice.

"Long as them consarn fools don't come pesticatin' around me," Booger said, "I don't mind 'em. The unholy trinity hates their guts, so old Booger reckons even a bad dog is worth a bone."

Booger belched again. "You boys wanna see me light a fart?"

"Let's not and say we did," Fargo told him.

"Say," Booger went right on, "we'll reach Victoria real soon now. That means sawdust floors and sparkling doxies. Course, pretty teeth here don't never pay for it like us ugly buzzards."

"Well, now," McDade said, lowering his voice, "speaking of that—look what the breeze is blowing our way, boyos."

Miranda and Katrina, both carrying their canvas camp chairs, were headed toward Fargo and the rest.

Booger snickered. "Push-push, eh, Fargo?" he said low in the Trailsman's ear.

"May we join you gentlemen?" Miranda inquired.

"Would a cow lick Lot's wife?" Booger replied, moving his ample bulk so that the two women could flank Fargo where he sat leaning back on his saddle.

"Skye," Miranda said, having recently begun to call him by his front name, "this place you mentioned, Victoria. Are there shops there?"

In the ruddy firelight she looked mighty fetching. A white cotton dress bared her perfect, slender shoulders, its deep décolletage revealing a tantalizing view of her high-thrusting breasts. In the flattering light, her sensual lips glowed with moisture, and the sculpted cheekbones made her seem like a fine painting come to life.

Fargo could have reached out and touched her, she sat so close. Her honeysuckle perfume filled his nostrils, and stirred heat in his loins.

"Not the kinds of shops you ladies probably have in mind. It's mostly an outfitting settlement like Powder-horn. There's plenty of good stores there, but most of them hawk trail supplies. You might find a few ladies' frills—hats and such. But, frankly, I'd advise you to stay away from the place. It's a mite rough."

She didn't seem that interested in her own question or his answer, and Fargo suspected it was just a feminine wile to cover another purpose. Suddenly she lowered her voice and whispered:

"You told me the ribbon is pretty, but what's in the package? Perhaps you'd like a little peek?"

She had strategically placed her chair so that the light caught her lap, which was just above Fargo's line of sight. Discreetly she opened her legs and tugged her dress up as if simply adjusting it under her. She wore nothing underneath.

Caught pleasantly by surprise, Fargo got a quick glance at the soft fur and early-morning dew of her belly mouth.

It lasted only a few seconds, but instantly hot blood exploded into Fargo's shaft, and he was forced to shift his position, his heartbeat throbbing like tom-toms in his ears.

Fargo glanced at Katrina and could have sworn she had caught this little erotic peep show. If so, she gave no sign.

Interesting, Fargo told himself.

But Diego Salazar stood not far off, his tunic unbuttoned for the night as he quaffed fine Madeira from a silver goblet. He seemed to realize something was afoot. He watched Fargo from a sullen deadpan, jealous rage smoldering within him.

"Ladies," he called over in his magisterial, overbearing tone, "the new day will begin early. Perhaps you should retire to your tent."

Miranda's pretty face set itself hard, and she was about to retort, but Katrina quickly spoke up.

"Yes, Miranda, Diego is right. You asked me to wash your hair tonight, remember?"

After the two women said good night and left, Booger couldn't resist antagonizing Salazar. He raised his voice.

"Yessir, boys, looks to old Booger like that pretty little muffin Miranda has struck a spark for Fargo. Yeah, boy, the Trailsman never gets woman hungry for long."

"Shut your cake hole, you big ape," Fargo muttered.

"You are a peasant, McTeague," Salazar said. "In my country, peasants do not speak so disrespectfully of their betters."

"Pitch it to hell, Sancho! Case you ain't noticed, you strutting peacock, this here is *my* country! You whip-dick sons a' bitches couldn't even hang on to Mexico, so don't start swingin' your eggs around here, you damn foreign toad eater."

Salazar visibly stiffened like a hound on point. "Perhaps we shall see just whose country it is, peasant. As they say, the worm will turn."

Fargo unfolded to his feet. "You wanna spell that out plain, Captain?"

Booger's angry, booming voice had brought Hernando Quintana hustling over. He sent Salazar a warning glance.

"Gentlemen," he addressed the Americans in a placating tone, "ignore Diego—sometimes his Castilian pride gets the better of his good sense. Of course we know whose country this is—the land rightfully wrested from the tyrant King George by your gallant Colonial army. An inspiration to oppressed men everywhere."

The conciliatory speech seemed to settle Booger's Irish, but Fargo found it oily and insincere. Salazar walked off to join his two companions, and Quintana returned to his tent.

Booger lowered his voice. "Fargo, I seen that little hussy give you a peek at her quim. Of course you must poke the little tart, but be careful you don't get shot in the whang."

"More coffee, peasants?" Deke said sarcastically.

Fargo held his cup out. But Salazar's queer remark just now would hound him for the rest of that night.

"Perhaps we shall see just whose country it is."

By the time a dull yellow sun broke over the Texas flatland, on the tenth morning of Fargo's latest job, Deke Lafferty had whipped up a delicious breakfast of eggs, fried potatoes, and pan bread.

Fargo carried two plates out to Cherokee Bob and All Behind Him, who had spread their blankets about fifty yards west of the main camp. Fargo kicked both of them awake.

"Up and on the line, you heathens." He greeted them. "Grub pile."

Cherokee Bob groaned as he struggled to sit up. "Katy Christ," the Shawnee managed in a cracked voice. "Somebody shot me in the head."

Fargo glanced at the empty whiskey bottle lying in the grass. "You two were out on the roof last night. Quit stealing Deke's liquor. You're supposed to be on picket guard, not serenading the rattlesnakes."

All Behind Him had already snatched a plate from Fargo's hand. He tossed the fork aside and began shoveling food into his mouth by hand.

"Damn good grub," he said with his mouth full. "You want yours?" he asked Bob.

"Take it. I think I'm gonna puke."

Fargo shook his head. "Yeah, the Noble Red Man. Look, this ain't Fiddler's Green. The Skinny Wolf could try a play anytime now. Keep your eyes peeled."

"We need horses," Cherokee Bob complained. "I ain't in no condition to walk thirty miles again today. Hell, my feet—"

"Put away your violin. I'll talk to Bitch about it," Fargo said. "But *don't* eat the damn things or I'll have to reimburse Quintana."

"Flip you for two bits," Cherokee Bob offered over his shoulder as he took a piss.

"Nix on that. I know all about your two-headed coin. You been eavesdropping on the guards like I told you?"

"Hell, it ain't easy, Fargo. These sons of Coronado ain't exactly sweet on Indians. If they catch me too close, they'll perforate my liver. Their Spanish is kinda queer, too—they don't talk like Mexicans, I can't make out all the sounds. Now and then I catch a word in the breeze. Especially *patria.*"

"Fatherland, right?"

Cherokee Bob nodded distractedly, staring downward in dismay. "Shit, something bit my dick last night."

"Never mind that. What else did you hear?"

"I hear *batalla* a lot, battle. And course they talk about women and stuff like that. Specially some pert skirt named Miranda. They all wanna screw her. That's the old man's daughter, ain't she?"

"Yeah. Well, keep listening," Fargo said.

By now All Behind Him had emptied both plates and was licking the grease from his fingers. He looked at Fargo. "Any more?"

Fargo was amazed at the Delaware's prodigious appetite. He took the plates back to camp, tossing them into Deke's wreck pan, a tub filled with soapy water. Fargo filled his own plate and squatted on his heels to eat.

"Salazar and his two boyfriends are on the warpath." Booger greeted him. "They're staring at us like they're measuring us for coffins. Let's kill those garlics right now before they plug us in the back."

"Mebbe Salazar seen his woman flash her goods at you last night, Fargo," Deke suggested.

Fargo stared at Booger. "Your tongue swings way too loose. What, are you the camp crier now?"

"I'm damned if I'll keep your dirty little secrets, Catfish. Damn, *look* at that ugly son of a bitch Rivera. He'd rob a church poor box."

"And you didn't when we were broke in Santa Fe?"

Booger averted his eyes. "Yeah, there was that. But at least I felt bad about it after."

"Bitch," Fargo said to McDade, "you got a couple of horses or mules those Indians can use?"

"Well, it's Quintana who bought all the stock. But then, he let you decide about taking on the Indians, so I reckon it's all right. I'll cut out two mules, but I got no saddles I can spare."

"They don't use saddles. Listen, all three of you. Something's on the spit, but I got no idea yet what it is. Keep a sharp eye out. Booger, *stop* roweling those soldiers. You push them too far and we'll be up Salt River. Twice now somebody's tried to blow out our lamps, and for all we know Salazar and his bootlicks could be in the mix without Quintana's permission."

Fargo finished breakfast and was halfway to the rope corral when a feminine voice behind him pulled him up short.

"Senor Fargo?"

He turned and saw Katrina Robles hurrying toward him. "A word with you, please?"

Fargo touched his hat brim. "There's always time to talk with pretty ladies, Miss Robles."

Those cherry red, sultry lips smiled at him. "I have heard how gallant you are with the ladies."

She glanced carefully around, then added, "May I speak frankly with you? *Very* frankly?"

Better and better, Fargo thought. "Please do. I like frankness in a woman."

"Last night around the fire—I saw what Miranda did to . . . tantalize you. In fact, I knew it would happen when she made up that silly excuse to ask you about shops along the route."

Fargo smiled. "Well, it was a pleasant surprise. She's a bold little thing, isn't she?"

"Yes . . . and no. She is not . . . stimulating you because she wants to have . . . intimate relations with you."

Fargo tugged at his short beard. "Hmm. She sure has an unusual way of saying she's not interested."

"Senor Fargo—"

"Skye."

"Skye, 'unusual' is the very word. I have been this young woman's duenna since her mother was taken seven years ago. She is both an exhibitionist and a voyeur. Are these words familiar to you?"

Fargo mulled that over. "I think I can figure out what you mean by the first one. That second word is too far north for me."

"Miranda is not a virgin. But actually having intimate relations with men she finds attractive—men such as you— does not satisfy her. Rather, as she did last night, she becomes excited by revealing her . . . feminine parts to the men of her choice in public where there is risk of being seen by others. It excites her more than the physical act of love."

Fargo was disappointed but impressed. He'd dallied with quite a gallery of unconventional women in his day: gals who liked to double-team him; one lass who liked to play rough with a riding crop; even one wild little cottontail up in the Rockies who insisted he do her in the saddle with the Ovaro at a full gallop. Nor could he forget the dangerous beauty in a hellhole called Hangtown, who suspended herself over him in a basket with a hole in the bottom, rigged so she could go up and down on his staff.

And Miranda Quintana, too, apparently measured corn by her own bushel.

"Well," he replied, "I guess a quick peek is better than a poke in the eye with a sharp stick. All right, that's an exhibitionist. So what's a voyeur?"

"That means she loves to watch the man she is attracted to have intimate relations with another woman while she stimulates herself with her fingers."

"Jesus. Does she supply the woman?" he said, half in jest, half in hope.

Katrina's flawless caramel-colored face deepened in a blush. "Yes. You are looking at her."

Fargo, caught flat-footed, went slack-jawed for a moment.

"Oh, I do not *always* agree to do it," she hastened to add.

"But in your case . . . and of course only if you approve of the idea."

A sudden surge of pounding blood uncoiled Fargo's man gland and plowed a huge furrow down one leg of his buckskins. Katrina's eyes widened as she watched it visibly throb with his heartbeat.

"*Aye Dios!*" she breathed in a voice just above a whisper. "*Es muy grande.* I see you *do* approve?"

Fargo swallowed audibly. "Oh, I surpass approval, Katrina. But this might be a little tricky. Captain Salazar watches her like a cat on a rat, and there's not exactly any privacy in this camp."

"Oh, there is," she assured him eagerly. "Every second night Miranda and I have the tent to ourselves for an entire hour while we bathe. Hernando joins Diego and the others, and he has issued strict orders that *no* men are allowed anywhere near the tent. You would have to be careful, of course, but it will be dark."

"What night do you have in mind?"

"Tonight is bath night," she replied, giving him a coy smile. "At eight o'clock our baths begin."

"Well, now," Fargo said. "Maybe I can hold the soap for you."

8

Fargo had intended, if he was ever alone with Katrina, to ply her with questions about Quintana and the rest of the Spaniards. However, after her surprise announcement about Miranda and what was coming up that very night, it didn't seem like the time to spoil the exciting mood.

That impending eight p.m. rendezvous in the tent with two beautiful wantons definitely promised to be the high point of his life since a pleasant erotic interlude a month earlier with a young widow up at Fort Smith. But he forced it from his mind in the interest of staying alive.

Several times, keeping Cherokee Bob and All Behind Him on the flanks, he scoured the Quintana party's back trail for signs they were being followed. With the pockets of thorny brush growing more frequent, he kept a constant eye on the Ovaro's ears, knowing they were his best chance of thwarting an ambush.

Fargo felt as if he were juggling lit dynamite. The Skinny Wolf, Salazar and his minions, the increasing chances of encountering warpath Kiowas and Comanches, perhaps even dangers posed by Hernando Quintana himself—potential trouble loomed from all sides, but the Trailsman still could not make the pieces of the puzzle fall into place.

"Damn it, old warhorse," he told the Ovaro at one point, frustration clear in his tone, "like my old trail pard Snowshoe Hendee used to say—I'm plumb exfluxuated."

It was close to midday and Fargo was about three miles behind the rest, eyes slitted against a hot, bright sun as they studied the ground. Ominously, he found the tracks of wild longhorns several times, but only once did he spot horse tracks not made by the Quintana party.

He reined in and swung down, squatting on his heels to study them. There were two sets, running north to south, made by iron-shod hooves.

Each print was only about three feet apart, meaning the horses were walking. He followed them south for about a mile and suddenly the prints were about nine feet apart—meaning the riders had gigged them up to a run.

But the edges of the prints were crumbling, so they were not recent. Owl hoots headed for the Rio Grande, he decided, forking leather again. Likely they were walking the horses to spell them.

As he pointed the Ovaro west again to catch up with the others, one fact plagued him above all others: assuming it was the Skinny Wolf's cutthroats who had dug the pitfall, and then given him and Booger a lead bath on the same day, how did they know Fargo was coming south unless they had an informant among the Quintana party, as the viceroy himself suggested? Was the spy just one maverick or an entire faction?

"Notice anything suspicious?" he asked, falling in beside the magnificent coach and keeping his voice low.

Booger shook his head. "Naw, but this is a stumper, Catfish. Old Booger had to change out the team *twice* today, once when the day was still a pup. Them's eight good, strong mules in the traces, and only the old man and the two gals riding inside."

Fargo lowered his voice even more. "It's got to be gold or silver—nothing else that heavy would be worth hiding. Well, he ain't the first wealthy man to haul a fortune with him."

"Uh-huh. But do you credit the old-timer's story about the Skinny Wolf being after his daughter?"

Fargo's eyes met Booger's. "No, I don't. It sounds all right when you first hear it, but once you think on it for a bit, it starts to smell funny. I see our sticks float the same way, old son. You're wondering how El Lobo found out about the money."

"You've placed the ax on the helve. It could be any one of these dagos, but I like Rivera for it."

"It's most likely him, Salazar, or Aragon," Fargo agreed. "They're most likely to know the old man's secrets. I count about fifteen more Spaniards besides the unholy trinity. You can call them workers or soldiers, but I'm guessing they're in the dark about whatever's hidden in the coach."

Miranda Quintana poked her well-shaped head outside the window.

"Two hale, hearty men like you," she teased, "yet all this schoolgirl whispering? May the rest of us know your secret?"

Fargo twisted around in the saddle and touched the brim of his hat. "We were just discussing what it is that makes Spanish women so beautiful."

"As for myself, Mr. Fargo, I am half American. In fact, much to Father's chagrin, I can barely speak Spanish. Of course," she added in a meaningful tone, "Katrina is a full-blooded Spaniard—and quite attractive. Don't you agree?"

"I do, indeed, Miss Quintana. We are fortunate to have two beautiful women along. An embarrassment of riches."

Quintana's silver head poked out. "You needn't flatter her, Senor Fargo. She is already vain enough. And just for the record, I am an American, too. I was granted dual citizenship by the governor of Louisiana."

"Sounds like you been hedging your bets," Booger tossed in. "Anyhow, some of your men don't seem to realize what country this is. They act like Coronado and that bunch are still the honchos."

"Nonsense, Mr. McTeague. They're just prideful."

"There's a good patch of graze coming up," Fargo said. "Might be a good spot to make a nooning."

"A good suggestion. Deke Lafferty is no New Orleans chef, but he is an excellent trail cook."

Forty minutes later Fargo was tying in to a plate of palatable stew made from canned beef, fresh potatoes, and desiccated vegetables. As usual, most of Quintana's men had taken their food off and formed a circle about a hundred feet away from Hernando Quintana and the ladies, who ate with Fargo and his companions.

Salazar, however, elected to eat with the Quintanas instead of his two uniformed minions. Booger and Fargo exchanged a knowing smirk, realizing that the pompous ass was seething with jealousy. He made a gallant show of forgoing his meal to hold Miranda's pongee parasol over her while she ate.

"You see, Mr. Fargo," she explained in a teasing lilt, "Diego has been steeped in the courtly love tradition of the Middle Ages—the true knight sacrifices his own comfort for that of his lady—or the woman he *thinks* is his lady."

Salazar's wire-tight lips shaped a frown at her remark.

"Nothing wrong with being attentive to a lady," Fargo said.

"No," she replied, sending him a sly smile, "there isn't, is there? Right, Katrina?"

Katrina's eyes met Fargo's, eyes filled with lustful promises.

"I have observed that American men," Salazar said with stiff formality, "treat their women like livestock."

"Actually, Captain," Bitch Creek McDade interjected in a polite tone, "we treat our livestock better than our women. A man's life doesn't generally depend on a woman."

"You can't butcher a decent steak off 'em, neither," Deke tossed in, and Booger laughed so hard that food exploded from his mouth.

"Oh, crikes! 'Scuze me, Captain," he said to Salazar with false contrition. "Did I soil your courtly pants?"

Deke pretended to cough to cover his laughter while Fargo, unable to suppress a grin himself, dug a warning elbow into Booger's ribs.

Just then a sudden, hard gust of wind sprang up, seemingly from nowhere. Fargo glanced up from his plate to watch one of the men in the circle, cheered on by his companions, dash out into the brush. He was pursuing his woven-straw hat, which was now hopping and sailing in the wind.

Fargo recognized the deep, angry bellowing the moment it began.

In a hollow drumbeat of charging hooves, an enraged wild longhorn materialized out of the brush, head lowered, at least six feet separating its two deadly horns.

The man never even had a chance to dodge. Both women screamed in horror when one of the horns punched clean through his stomach, shoving bloody, convoluted entrails out his back and swooping him off the ground.

The man's high-pitched cry of inexpressible pain raised the fine hairs on the back of Fargo's neck. The wild longhorn gave a mighty shake of his head, dislodging the annoying weight from his horn. It took the young Spaniard's nervous system a few seconds to register the final fact of death. And during that brief time the dying man's heels scratched at the dirt like frantic claws.

This was over in a few heartbeats, everyone so shocked by the unexpected death that no one moved except Fargo—not even when the enraged man killer thundered straight for the group nearest the chuck wagon, perhaps incited by Miranda's scarlet shawl.

Fargo's Henry lay grounded at his feet. He tossed his plate and snatched up the rifle, dropping into a kneeling-offhand position. Fargo worked the lever and pressed the stock to his shoulder, his cheek to the brass. Only a head shot would drop a man killer riled up like this one, so he made sure of his bead before squeezing off a round.

The Henry kicked hard into his shoulder and a curly rope of blood erupted from the longhorn's head before it crashed to the ground, momentum making it skid a few yards more.

Gray-white smoke was still curling from the Henry's muzzle when the real threat was unleashed.

"Madre de Dios!" Quintana exclaimed when at least half a dozen more *ladinos* charged from the brush.

The men in the farther circle had already scattered in panic, only a few of them having enough presence of mind to shoot at the beasts, with little effect. And now the *ladinos* hurtled toward the smaller group near the chuck wagon like inexorable juggernauts of death.

"Booger!" Fargo shouted. "Up and on the line!"

Deadly accuracy and rapid fire were their only hope now. Again, again, yet again the Henry bucked in Fargo's hands, joined by the sharp cracks of Booger's North & Savage. The last man-killing longhorn came within twenty feet of goring Fargo before he shot it dead.

Salazar, who had been utterly useless during the harrowing attack, now did one useful thing: he caught Miranda when she suddenly went pale and passed out.

Quintana removed a handkerchief tucked into his sleeve and patted his perspiring brow.

"Senor Fargo, you have earned every dollar I paid you by your quick actions just now. You also, Senor McTeague."

He gave Salazar a reproving glance. "And you, Diego—a graduate of the Colegio Militario, onetime *comandante* of the Royal Barracks, and you merely stood there like a pillar of salt?"

Fargo tried to pour oil on troubled waters. "You can't expect him to carry his rifle at all times in camp, don Hernando, and his sidearm would've been useless."

"Perhaps that is true. And certainly Diego is no coward. But you were right all along about these wild cattle, and now we will have to bury poor Antonio in a forsaken grave. Do you see now, Diego, why I hired this man? You mocked him when he warned us. Your military training is second to none, but you and your men are not frontiersmen."

Salazar shot Fargo a spiteful glance. "There were many frontiersmen at the Alamo battle, don Hernando, but Antonio Santa Anna, a military man, defeated them."

"And what good," Quintana countered, "did the Alamo victory do for Mexico? Not too many years later she lost almost half her country to the Americans."

This petty quarreling was wasted on Fargo, but one impression struck him full force: when Hernando Quintana made that last comment about losing country to the Americans, his tone had suddenly spiked with anger and resentment. What had begun as a dressing-down of Captain Salazar ended up as a bitter complaint against a nation.

Interesting, Fargo thought.

Mighty damn interesting. . . .

"Fargo, you damn piker!" Booger exclaimed. "It's damn near time to turn in and you've put on your clean buckskins. And you're scrubbing your teeth. You're gonna get some poon, ain'tcher?"

"At least pre*tend* you've got more brains than a rabbit," Fargo scoffed, still working his teeth with a hog-bristle brush.

"You *are*, you sneaky son of a bitch. You're grinnin' like a possum eatin' a yellow jacket. That's your Fargo's-gonna-get-some grin. Which one will you prong tonight, Miranda or Katrina?"

"Neither one," Fargo lied. "I am going to visit the ladies,

sure, but only to ask them some questions, maybe see if I can find out—"

"Serve it on toast! Fargo, when it comes to pretty lasses, you're a one-eyed dog in a meat factory. You're shaggin' one a' them gals."

"Where?" Fargo demanded. "The entire camp is lit up like a widow's front parlor. There's eyes and ears everywhere."

"Why, in that fancy circus tent, that's where. The viceroy just left with Salazar."

"Uh-huh, in the tent. Do you really believe I'm gonna bull one of the women while the other watches? Or do you figure I'm gonna poke both of them turnabout?"

The sun had set an hour earlier and a vast Texas sky was peppered silver with glimmering stars. Booger, already stretched out on his blankets, mulled that question over.

"Nah, that don't seem likely even for you. I screwed a whore one time in Cheyenne while another one watched, but she was holding a gun on me case I got rough. Miranda and Katrina is what you call the Quality."

"You just listen close while I'm gone. Cherokee Bob will give you the wolf howl if the Indians spot anything."

Fargo did the best he could to avoid the flickering torch-light as he crossed to the center of camp, keeping his eyes to all sides. Deke and Bitch Creek McDade had already turned in, and the Spaniards were either on night guard or gathered around a distant fire.

What, Fargo wondered, did they talk about when the Americans weren't around to hear them?

He ducked through the fly of the tent and immediately smelled the pleasant odor of femininity—a tantalizing concoction of cologne, fancy perfumed soaps, and the faint, damp-earth smell of their sex.

The inside of the huge tent was softly lighted by several lanterns. Screened panels divided the tent roughly in two, one side now filled by two wooden bathtubs, still steaming. Fargo saw women's clothing heaped near the tubs, but no sign of the women themselves.

"Evening, ladies," he called out in a low voice. "All right if I come in?"

"We're over here, Skye," answered a silvery-smooth, musical lilt he recognized as Miranda's voice.

Fargo ducked around to the left side of the panel, then forgot to take his next breath. He was gazing upon a powerfully erotic scene right out of the myth of the Isle of Lesbos.

"Well, hell-*o*," he greeted the two nymphs, instantly so hard that a pup tent sprang up in the front of his trousers.

Each woman lay, bare-butt naked, on a low, backless couch covered with crisp white linen sheets, their heads resting on fancy satin pillows, their hair unrestrained and fanned out like rich manes.

"Which one of us do you like best?" Miranda demanded. "Take a good look."

Fargo did. Miranda's hair was chestnut with blond streaks, Katrina's the rich, shiny black of a raven's wings; Miranda's sleepy-lidded, languid eyes were purple-black like the juice of dark berries, Katrina's intense and the color of dark mahogany; Miranda's lips were heart-shaped and pouting, Katrina's full and sultry; Miranda's tits were smaller but hard, with pointy nipples ending in strawberry tips, Katrina's tits heavier and pendant, the nipples like cocoa.

Miranda still showed the coltish figure of a young woman of perhaps nineteen or twenty, slim-hipped and leggy, her stomach flat. Katrina, perhaps ten years older, had the voluptuous figure of a woman in her prime, with flaring hips and a gently rounded stomach. Miranda's mons bush was silkier and sparse, Katrina's like a mat of dark wool.

Fargo swallowed audibly as he unbuckled his gun belt.

"Which one do I like best? Ladies, all I see are two art masterpieces."

"That bulge in your pants is breathtaking," Miranda marveled. "Did you stick a pair of socks down there to impress us? Let's see what you've *really* got."

Fargo dropped his trousers and both women goggled at the blue-veined beast now unleashed. It had been too long for Fargo, and each pounding beat of his excited heart made his swollen manhood leap like a jittery divining rod.

"My *stars!*" Miranda gasped. "Katrina, have you *ever*

seen size like that on a man? Look at his sac! Those aren't nuts—they're apples!"

"Oh, he will fill me up like no man has," Katrina said, her voice husky with the hunger of lust.

"Kneel between her legs, Skye," Miranda said, one slim hand sliding between her own legs. "But do everything I tell you, all right? Don't touch me, but I want you to look at me a lot while you do her, understand?"

"Lady's choice," Fargo assured her. Katrina opened her legs wide and Fargo knelt between them.

"Kiss her valentine," Miranda directed.

Fargo lowered his face into the steamy grotto of Katrina's sex, teasing her clitty out of its sheath with a probing tongue.

"Eso, sí!" Katrina groaned, her hips shimmying. "Just like that!"

A minute of this treatment had Katrina hotter than a branding iron and panting like a dog in August.

"Now stick your thingie between her tits," Miranda ordered.

Fargo obligingly moved higher as Katrina grabbed her breasts and parted them for him. Fargo parked his curved saber in the warm, velvet-smooth valley. Katrina began rolling him between her tits, faster and faster, sending pulses of hot, tickling pleasure back to Fargo's groin.

"Look at me, Skye!" Miranda commanded, her voice rising an octave in her excitement and sense of total control. "See what I'm doing?"

Her thighs were parted wide and she was using two fingers to tease her sensitive pearl. Fargo could see "the little man in the boat" was already swollen with her passion.

"Stick it in her now, Skye!" Miranda half ordered, half begged. "Do her fast and hard!"

Fargo had never been one for taking orders, but these commands were pure pleasure. He moved back down and placed his hands under Katrina's firm, full ass, lifting her and sliding his staff in deep. The pliant, slick walls of her sex opened for him, tight and accommodating at the same time.

"Aye Dios!" Katrina gasped, pumping on his length. "Miranda, his tool is perfect! Oh, Skye, *eso, sí . . .*!"

Fargo pounded the saddle harder and faster, forcing Katrina to smother her uncontrollable cries into a pillow.

"*Look* at me!" Miranda ordered again, her fingers moving in a blur of speed now, her face deeply flushed.

A few moments later it was a three-ring extravaganza: Miranda doubled up, gasping hard, as a string of climaxes racked her body; Katrina screamed into the pillow as Fargo took her over the final pinnacle; and a few seconds later he exploded hard inside her, needing seven or eight conclusive thrusts to spend himself.

All three lay in dazed lassitude for uncounted minutes, their heart rates and breathing only slowly returning to normal. It was Miranda who broke the silence.

"There's still plenty of time, Skye," she said, "before Father returns. Do you think you could go again?"

"Go again?" Katrina repeated. "Look! He never got soft after the first one!"

"Wonderful! Now, Skye, I want you to watch me as you stick it in Katrina's mouth. . . ."

9

Two days after Fargo's unforgettable interlude in the tent, El Lobo Flaco gathered his men around him in the shelter of a draw between two low hills.

A healthy respect for the danger represented by this gringo Skye Fargo, who was known to toss a wide loop when he scouted, had kept the Skinny Wolf well to the south of the Quintana party. But thanks to their informant's mirror signals and occasional written messages, they knew the party's rate of progress, disposition of sentries, camp procedures—and Fargo's daily patterns.

"We cannot, as I had hoped, win over the viceroy's people," El Lobo reported. "Not at the present. Miguel assured me this pretty soldier, Salazar, is a dog loyal to his master. So are the rest. These idealistic Spanish loyalists believe in Quintana's wild scheme. And true believers can be dangerous, indeed—they place their precious cause above fear of death."

"Is it truly a wild scheme, *jefe*?" spoke up Ramon Velasquez, the Skinny Wolf's *segundo* or second in charge.

El Lobo's skullish face looked sinister in the brassy early-morning light.

"You keep asking me this as if it matters to us. *De veras*, Ramon, it is perhaps well thought out and well timed. The gringos have a nasty civil war on their hands. If enough of the Spanish devils in *Californio* join them, *pues quien sabe*—then who knows?"

"With so many silver bars, enough *will* join them, *jefe*," said the blade expert named Paco.

The Skinny Wolf thought about that and nodded. "Yes. And if all else fails, *we* could pretend to offer our guns to their cause. This *viejo*, this old man Quintana could use good killers like us, huh? But this can never happen while the Trailsman is above the earth."

"Then why is he?" spoke up Pedro Montoya, one of the men who had hauled the dismembered corpse of the Papago Indian girl and left it along the Southwest Trail. "We should have sent him to his ancestors by now."

"*Oye, necio*—listen, you fool. The road to hell is paved with the bones of men who underrated Fargo. You do not grasp this because you were not with us at the Pecos River when he killed three of my men and nearly killed me."

"I was there, Pedro," Velasquez put in. "He is cunning, resourceful, and has the courage of a she-grizz protecting her cubs."

"Trying to kill him in open country like this," the Skinny Wolf said, "is a fool's errand now that we have failed once. He is alerted. But they will reach Victoria by this evening, and that is where we will kill him. Fargo, it is true, likes to seek out the emptiest corner of the canyon. But he also likes saloons. He likes his beer, his poker games, and because he will not likely *chinga* the viceroy's daughter or her shapely duenna, he will want a woman. Victoria is known for its fine and willing whores."

Velasquez said, "You have a plan?"

El Lobo flashed his lipless grin. "A *plan*? Ramon, against Fargo, the mouse that has but one hole is quickly taken."

He looked at Pedro. "You are breathing fire to kill him. He has never seen you, so you are going to be waiting in the saloon, apparently in a stupor from drink, when he arrives. You will be disguised as a poor, broken-down, and unarmed *bracero*. A man who is already drunk and nodding out when Fargo arrives will not draw the attention of a man who comes in after he does."

"But, *jefe*, there are two saloons in Victoria, the Alibi and the Three Sisters. How will we know which one he selects?"

The Skinny Wolf assumed a pious look. "You have not heard? What a pity it is! Last night there was a terrible and mysterious fire. It burned the Three Sisters to the ground, eh, Paco?"

"*Sí, jefe*, a very tragic fire. Now there is only one saloon."

The rest of the men laughed.

"But *ten cuidado*, Pedro. Be very careful. We will talk

74

more about this, but if it becomes necessary you must strike swift and sure and escape before the big ape with Fargo recovers his senses. However, if all goes well you may never have to make your move."

"The second mouse hole you spoke of?" Velasquez asked.

The Skinny Wolf nodded. "*Preciso.* Fargo likes his beer, but tonight there will be no beer. Only whiskey. I know the bartender at the Alibi—he is a gringo, but a greedy one who would sell his own mother to the Devil for a gold piece. I am going to ride ahead to Victoria now and make an arrangement with him. I swear by Jesus Christ and all the saints that Fargo has seen his last sunrise."

"Deke," Booger said as the cook spooned biscuit dough onto a flat iron baking pan, "where the hell does them two gals take their bath?"

"Right in their tent."

Booger shot a homicidal stare at Fargo, who sat nearby with a look of cherubic innocence on his weather-bronzed face. He ran bore patches through both of his weapons and coated the firing mechanisms lightly with gun oil.

"Ah? In their tent, is it?"

"Sure. Every other night I heat up the water for 'em. The old man goes off with Salazar and them while the women scrub up. Oh, to be a fly on them canvas walls, huh?"

"Every other night, you say?"

"I don't believe I spoke Chinee," Deke said irritably. "Tonight I'll be heatin' water again."

"Fargo, you treacherous son of a bitch," Booger said in a low, dangerous voice. "That means when you went *visiting* night before last, it was their bath night. I *knew* you came back smelling like fish! A night of unbridled lust for the Trailsman while old Booger stroked his wand."

Hearing this, Deke perked up. "So you pitched a little hay, Skye? One 'r both?"

"Oh, slyboots never tells," Booger carped. "He just eats the whole of the meat and leaves old Booger the parsley."

"Ease off," Fargo said, "or at least set it to a tune. I ain't your damn pimp. Besides, you'll be in Victoria tonight and you can get your ashes hauled."

This remark heartened Booger. "Say, that's the straight! And there's some fine, smoke-eyed soiled doves there."

Bitch Creek McDade joined the group and poured himself some coffee.

"Looks like we'll be going in, too, Deke. I talked to Mr. Quintana last night. He said all four of us could go because he's keeping all his men in camp."

"A wise policy," Fargo said. "A Spaniard is a Mexican to a Texan. Victoria tolerates local Mexers and even a stray stranger, but that whole bunch arriving in one night would trigger a ruckus. Lead *would* fly."

"You know, Catfish," Booger said to Fargo, "that old viceroy looks plenty healthy to me, if you catch my drift?"

Fargo caught it, all right, and he had noticed the same thing. He'd had twelve days now to watch Quintana, a man supposedly moving to California to salvage his health. The Spaniard seemed hale and healthy, and Fargo hadn't heard him cough even once.

"Look at Rivera watching us," McDade said. "He hates all of us, especially Booger."

"That gimlet-eyed bastard is crazy, Bitch," Deke said. "You can see it in his eyes, most especial when he looks at Booger."

"I'm glad he hates me," Booger said calmly, "on account I mean to kill him. That son of de Soto is already dead and don't know it."

Deke banged the triangle mounted on the tailgate of the chuck wagon. "Grub pile! Come and get it 'fore I toss it to the birds!"

As usual Fargo heaped up two plates and headed south of camp to feed Cherokee Bob and All Behind Him. The sun had risen high enough to show how much the terrain had changed since they had set out from Powder-horn on the Gulf Coast. The Texas flatland had given way to ravines and low chaparral hills surrounding them, unfolding toward the far horizon in brown waves. The scalloped silhouette of more formidable hills lay ahead to the west.

"Christ." Fargo greeted the Indians, surprised. "You two are sober as deacons. So you've stopped stealing the medicine whiskey?"

"Stopped, my ass," Cherokee Bob grumbled. "That bandy-legged cook has got damn good at hiding it."

All Behind Him snatched a plate from Fargo. As usual, he tossed the fork aside and shoveled the food in by hand.

"Seems to me he used to talk more," Fargo remarked.

"He's lost all his teeth since you seen us last," Cherokee Bob explained. "He don't make much sense when he talks now."

"Lost all his teeth and he's eating bacon that fast?"

"Oh, he can chew like a spring-drunk beaver. See, we was hungry and stole a government mule at Fort Union. But this stupid Delaware got behind it, and it fetched him a kick that knocked him out for two days. Knocked his last teeth out, too. So one night he got drunk as a fiddler's bitch and took a horseshoe rasp to his gums. Scraped 'em clear down to the jawbone. Now he just sorta crushes and mashes his food."

"I'll be damn," Fargo said. "Scraped his own gums off?"

"Stone cold. Fargo, it was a bloody mess. But now he can crack walnuts open in his mouth. If he's really hungry, he just chews it all up shells and all."

Amazed, Fargo shook his head. "Any trouble last night?" he asked.

"Not so's you'd notice. That pig Rivera does spend plenty of time riding outside camp. I s'pose, being the sergeant, he's checking on the picket guards. But there was this queer sorta deal a couple nights ago."

Fargo looked annoyed. "A couple nights ago? Why didn't you mention it to me?"

Cherokee Bob, busy eating, just shrugged.

Fargo was damned if he would ever figure out the Indian mind. "Well, what happened?" he demanded.

"Cost you a dollar to find out. We ain't on wages, you know."

Fargo expelled a long sigh of surrender and fished a gold dollar out of his pocket, flipping it to the Shawnee. "All right, give."

"It was Rivera. Around midnight he ducked into this big clump of brush. I figured maybe he was taking a shit. But he wasn't in there long enough. Next morning I poked around in there. Didn't find anything, though."

"How 'bout tracks?"

"Them I found. Boot prints coming from the south, then

heading back that way. I followed 'em south for about a mile and seen where a horse had been waiting. Those tracks went south, too, but I wasn't stupid enough to follow. Could be Rivera left a note in that brush for somebody to pick up."

"Interesting," Fargo said.

"Yeah, well, something else is interesting, too—them two big military guns these Spanish devils are hauling in that wagon. Bitch McDade says they're for scaring off Indians. You b'lieve that?"

"I got no evidence to the contrary," Fargo said.

"I got no evidence that birds can't fly to the moon, neither, but I doubt if they can."

"The hell's that s'pose to mean?"

"I ain't sure. It just seemed like the thing to say."

"Damned Indians," Fargo muttered, turning to leave. But Cherokee Bob called out behind him.

"Hey, can me and All Behind Him ride into Victoria with you tonight?"

Fargo turned back around. "Why? They won't serve liquor to Indians. More likely, they'll shoot you full of holes."

"Yeah, but I know this one whore there. Her name's Margarita. She works her own crib on the edge of town, and she'll strap on an Indian buck if we pay her double. Fargo, we ain't had no pussy for a helluva long time."

"You mean that toothless Delaware actually stops eating long enough to get a poke?"

"I like fuck." All Behind Him spoke up, belching loudly before licking the grease from his plate.

Fargo gave in. "Well, I guess it's only fair. It'll be dark when we ride in. Besides, it just might be a good idea to have you two lurking in the shadows. El Lobo hasn't tried to put the quietus on me in almost a week. But he won't waste this opportunity tonight."

"He sure's hell won't," Cherokee Bob agreed. "Before this night is over, somebody is going to die hard."

Fargo halted the Quintana party an hour before sundown on the bank of a creek about two miles east of the settlement of Victoria, a rustic but bustling place that served mainly as a supply center for travelers along the Southwest Trail.

"Fargo, is your garret furnished?" Booger demanded when he found out the two Indians would be riding along with the four white men into Victoria. "That damn Cherokee Bob could get us all killed pulling one of his damn rooks."

"You're more likely to get us killed, you crazy bastard. Just pipe down. Those two aren't as stupid as you look."

Fargo tightened the cinch and inspected the latigos before turning the stirrup and forking leather. Booger already sat atop his saddle ox. Bitch Creek McDade had cut out two horses for himself and Deke, and Fargo whistled sharply to the Indians as the four men gigged their horses toward town.

Cherokee Bob and All Behind Him fell in behind the men, riding the mules McDade had lent them.

"Them two are a hoot," Deke said. "But gol*dang* that Cherokee Bob's chewed-off ear is ugly. Puts me off my feed every time I look at it."

"Hey, McTeague!" Cherokee Bob called out. "Bet you five dollars I can tell you where you got that big ox."

"I'm in a crosswise mood, savage," Booger called back, "and I'd just as lief shoot you as look at you. No parlor tricks, hear?"

Booger lowered his voice. "That red son won't be happy until I ain't got two nickels left to rub together."

Deke chuckled. "That coy red bastard."

"Let me warn all three of you," Fargo said. "Those two Indians act like a pair of dance hall fops. But if you ever hear one of them say 'crick' and the other answer 'crack,' get the hell out of their way."

"Why?" McDade asked. "What do crick and crack mean?"

"It means anything too close to them might get killed, that's what. Those two are hell on four sticks when they choose to be. Mister, I mean grizzly bear dangerous."

Booger howled with mirth. "Dangerous? Them two pogies? Fargo, you're off your chump."

"I did my duty and warned you," Fargo said. "You best harken and heed. And speaking of danger—Booger, you saw what the Skinny Wolf and his murdering jackals did to that Indian girl. All of you have to keep a sharp eye out in Victoria. The Skinny Wolf *will* have some fox play to spring on us."

"I got my Colt Pocket Model," Deke said, "but I couldn't hit a bull in the butt with a banjo. I shot at a mad dog once and the bullet flew wide and killed a donkey."

"I don't even own a gun," McDade admitted. "All I got's a buck knife."

"You can both still keep your eyes open," Fargo said. "That's the main mile. Booger and me will take care of the fireworks."

"And how," Booger boasted. "Us two been in shooting frays from Old Mexico to the high Rockies. Left our share of widows and orphans, too."

Fifteen minutes later the riders crested a low hill and Victoria loomed into view in the grainy half-light of early evening. It was a good-sized cluster of unpainted wooden structures in a cup-shaped hollow. Enough light remained to show a still-smoldering, charred heap next to a sprawling mercantile.

"Well, I'll be et fir a tater!" Deke exclaimed. "The Three Sisters has burnt to the ground!"

"*Just* burned, too," Fargo added. "You can still smell it."

"Now, ain't that the drizzlin' shits?" Booger complained. "That was my favorite of the two watering holes when I used to whip a swift wagon through these parts. The Alibi ain't got no free lunch counter and lets too many beaners in. Their soiled doves wash your dick first, too, and if you cook off they charge for a full ride, the besotted slatterns."

While Booger carried on, however, Fargo was thoughtful. That saloon had gone up only in the past day or so. Fires were mighty common on the frontier, all right, but the Trailsman had never been a big believer in coincidences—especially not when the Skinny Wolf was in the mix.

"All right, you two reprobates," Fargo called back to Cherokee Bob and All Behind Him. "Both of you stay back until it gets a little darker. And for Christ sakes, watch your ampersands."

"Fargo, you're the one better worry," Cherokee Bob assured him. "El Lobo don't care a frog's fat ass 'bout a couple of shit-heel Injins. *You're* the jasper he's after, and I'll guarandamntee there's a trap waiting for you down there."

"I hope so," Fargo replied cheerfully. "Best way to cure a boil is to lance it."

10

The dusty main street of Victoria was nearly deserted when the four riders tied off their mounts in front of the Alibi. The saloon was a low, split-slab building with a shake roof and a long hitch rail out front still covered with bark. Nearly transparent hides, riddled with bullet holes, had been stretched over the windows to keep out the flies.

"Ain't exactly Delmonico's," Deke quipped.

Fargo stood in the rapidly darkening street for a full minute, looking carefully around for the telltale signs of an ambush and the best places for gunmen to lurk in the shadows.

"All right," he said. "I'm going in first with Booger behind me. Deke, you and Bitch stay just outside the door until I give you the hail."

Fargo slapped open the batwings and stepped inside. Stinking lard-oil lamps, suspended from overhead beams, cast an oily yellow light and made the few occupants look jaundiced.

The bartender was a tall, thin, hatchet-faced man with a spade beard and thinning red hair plastered down with axle grease.

"Evening, gents." He greeted them.

"Ha-ho, ha-ho!" Booger's voice boomed like a six-pounder. "Kill the women and rape the horses! Booger McTeague is here to drink, fuck, and fight, and the order does not matter!"

Fargo's eyes prowled the flyblown saloon. Only a few men stood at the plank bar, young men with sunburned faces and the scarred leather chaps of that new Texas breed known as cowboys. Predictably, they ignored Fargo and stared in slack-jawed amazement at Booger as if a house had suddenly walked in.

A few listless, jaded-looking soiled doves sat around a

table at the rear of the saloon, playing poker for bung-town coppers. They studied Fargo with close interest.

Fargo, however, was intently watching a lone Mexican apparently asleep at a table in the center of the room. He wore the white cotton clothing and rope sandals of a common *bracero*, his straw Sonora hat pulled low over his forehead.

To all appearances he was just a Mexican sleeping off a drunk, not an uncommon sight. But Fargo had survived so long on the frontier by trusting the sixth sense born of adversity. Besides, he was certain the Skinny Wolf had not given up on killing him.

"Booger," Fargo muttered, "keep your eyes on that bar dog and the rest while I roust this Mexer. I don't like the way both of his hands are hidden under that serape."

Circling around behind the Mexican to avoid making himself a target, Fargo moved up behind his chair and shucked out his Colt.

"Mite warm today to be wearing that serape inside, ain't it?" Fargo said loudly behind him.

The Mexican did not move or speak, continuing to snore.

Fargo screwed the muzzle of his Colt into the nape of the Mexican's neck. "I asked you a question, Pancho. But all I'm hearing is crickets."

This time the man stirred, his head swinging slowly up. "*No hablo ingles.*"

Fargo switched to Spanish. "*Hace mucho calor hoy. Por que tiene usted un serape?*"

"Mexicans always wear their serapes," the man replied in Spanish. "Hot or cold."

That was true enough. But Fargo was only interested in those hidden hands.

He tried English again. "Put both of your hands on the table."

"*No hablo ingles.*"

Fargo's Spanish was limited, but again he cobbled together the sentence. "*Ponen sus manos sobre la mesa.*"

There was a long pause while everyone in the saloon held their collective breath in suspense. The Mexican sat still as a granite block.

Fargo pressed the muzzle of the Colt even tighter. The Mexican's empty left hand emerged.

"*Y el otro,*" Fargo said. "*Lentemente.* Slowly."

Another long, almost painful silence. The right hand finally emerged gripping a Colt Navy revolver. The Mexican laid it on the table.

"Bitch, c'mon in!" Fargo called over his shoulder. "We just got you a sidearm. Deke, stay on watch outside the door. Watch my stallion's ears."

"Kill that sneaky little cockroach, Skye." Booger spoke up.

"I got a right to protect myself," the Mexican protested in English. "These *Tejanos* around here hate my people."

"Your language skills have improved dramatically," Fargo pointed out.

"Burn him where he sits, Fargo," Boomer urged. "The Skinny Wolf sent him to ventilate both of us."

"I have never heard of this Skinny Wolf," the Mexican insisted.

"That makes you the only swinging dick in these parts who hasn't," Fargo assured him.

He whipped the serape aside and patted the would-be assassin down, looking for a hideout gun.

By now Booger was wiggling in exasperation. "S'matter, Pretty Teeth? Have you been grazing loco weed? Burn him now or I will!"

"Ease off, Booger. He planned to plug us, all right. But this is an organized state, not a territory. You can't just send a man over the mountains because of what he had planned. He has to make his play first."

"Why, you damn Quaker!" Booger said in a disgusted tone.

"I prefer to send you back to El Lobo," Fargo told the Mexican. "You tell him Skye Fargo is gonna leave him drawing flies just like he did to that Indian girl, savvy?"

The Mexican revolved halfway around in his chair and sent Fargo a surly glance. "I do not know—"

"Shut your filthy sewer and clear out of here while I'm still in a cheerful mood."

"You cannot simply take a man's gun. As you say, I did not try to kill you."

Fargo dug into his pocket, then planked four gold quarter

eagles on the table. "There's ten bucks. You just sold that gun. Now light a shuck."

"But my gun—"

The noise seemed obscenely loud when Fargo cocked his short iron. His smile—all lips, no mirth—goaded the Mexican to raise one more objection.

The man wisely accepted his fate and scooped up the gold cartwheels. He left without another word, ambling out slowly to save some face.

"Make sure he rides out of town, Deke," Fargo called toward the door. "Bitch, come get your new firearm."

"Mister," one of the cowboys spoke up, "didn't that big fellow call you Fargo? Would that be Skye Fargo, the hombre they call the Trailsman?"

"Pah!" Booger spat into the dust, still disgusted with the Quaker. "In a pig's ass! The Trailsman has a set on him. *This* is Little Miss Pink Cheeks."

"Little Miss Pink Cheeks," the cowboy repeated, his face confused. "And he called that redheaded jasper Bitch? Pete, pour me another one, and less glass this time. I ain't drunk enough to make sense of it."

"The Mexer has skedaddled," Deke reported from outside the batwings.

"C'mon in and bend your elbow," Fargo said, leathering his shooter and heading toward the bar.

"What's yours?" the barkeep asked him.

"His Muleishness here," Fargo said, nodding toward Booger, "will have whiskey."

"Forty-rod, Bottles," Booger qualified. "And slop it over the brim. I drink nothing but Indian burner."

"And I'll have a beer," Fargo said. "Draw it nappy."

"Sorry. No barley pop today, Fargo."

Fargo felt a stab of disappointment. His mouth felt as stale as the last cracker in the bottom of the barrel, and he'd been thinking about a beer all day.

"That's a mite queer," he said. "Victoria has always had plenty of beer, and I saw the brewing house when we rode in."

The bartender shrugged indifferently. "Guess they ran out."

"You wouldn't think so," Fargo remarked, "what with the Three Sisters burning down."

Fargo felt a little prickle of alarm. The Three Sisters going up in flames, a killer lurking here, no beer in a town with its own brewery. . . . It was the Skinny Wolf's way to hedge his bets, and something in this barkeep's manner struck Fargo as off-kilter.

"Hold off on that forty-rod," Fargo said as the bartender reached toward the bottom shelf. "I'll take the rest of that bottle of Kentucky bourbon—the one you just poured out of for that waddie."

"That's top shelf. The bottle will cost you four dollars."

Fargo planked a shiner. "Sold. We'll need four jolt glasses, too."

"Fargo," Booger threatened, "p'r'aps a rap on the snoot will civilize you? You know I drink naught but popskull. That sissy piss don't even give old Booger a glow."

"Not that one," Fargo said when the barkeep reached for another bottle. "The one you just poured out of."

"You paid for a full bottle."

"I'm partial to the one you poured from," Fargo said.

"Mister, what's your dicker with me? It's all one."

"Humor me," Fargo said. "I'm eccentric."

Scowling, the bartender thumped down the bottle and four glasses.

"Tell you what," Fargo said amiably, "that bottle you were about to give me—have a jolt from it on me."

"I never touch the stuff except to pour it."

"Have a jolt from that bottle and I'll give you ten dollars."

"I never touch the—"

"Twenty dollars," Fargo said, his tone hardening.

By now tension again marked the air, and every man and soiled dove in the saloon was watching and listening expectantly. Booger suddenly caught on.

"Ha-ho," he said softly, "this one's coy as a French tart, ain't he?"

"Take a jolt from that bottle," Fargo repeated.

"I've had enough of your high-handed shit," the bartender said.

He pulled aside one half of his rawhide vest, revealing a star pinned to his shirt. "I'm a sheriff's deputy in Victoria, and nobody gives me orders except the sheriff and the judge. I let you run that Mexican out, but you're not pushing white men around."

Fargo looked at the cowboy who had spoken to him earlier. "Is he really a star packer or just flashing one?"

"He's sworn in, Mr. Fargo. But mainly he's just the tax collector, and he collects a lot more than he turns in."

"You ever seen him drink whiskey?"

"Can't say that I have. But I'm here to tell you—for twenty dollars I'd drink a cup of hot piss and demand seconds."

"All right, Deputy," Fargo surrendered, grabbing the bottle and handing the glasses to his companions. "I don't push when a thing won't move."

Fargo selected a table in the middle of the saloon. "Deke, watch that front door close. Bitch, you cover the back. Me and Booger will keep an eye on that bar dog."

"Hell, Fargo," Deke said, "you think that hatchet-faced son of a buck tried to poison us?"

"No bout adoubt it, Deke. The Skinny Wolf struck terms with him. Ain't squat we can do about it, though. The law is crooked here, and I don't plan to push this deal any further. Hanging rope is cheap in Texas."

Booger poured a drink, knocked it back, and loosed a string of curses. "Faugh! Fargo, you just got screwed with your pants on! Four dollars? This whiskey has been baptized."

McDade tasted it. "It's not watered down, Booger. You're just not used to the smooth stuff."

"Speaking of gettin' screwed, Booger," Deke said, leering toward the sporting girls at the rear of the saloon, "which one of them hoors catches your fancy?"

Booger, still in a stew over being forced to drink mild whiskey, scowled darkly.

"Stand 'em on their heads naked and they *all* look like sisters. The catfish here screws the Quality, and look at the dishrags old Booger gets. Well, a hungry dog must eat dirty pudding."

"Sorry, boys. No pudding tonight," Fargo said. "Not while the Skinny—"

"Watch it, Fargo!" a female voice shouted.

Fargo had carelessly taken his eye off the bartender. As he

instantly dived for the floor, he glanced toward the bar just as two barrels of a sawed-off Greener belched smoke and flame.

Fargo felt a burning sting like rattlesnake fangs. But the soiled dove's warning had come in the nick of time to avoid the brunt of the pellets. Fargo's empty chair splintered. He hit the floor hard on his left shoulder, shucking out his Colt.

The gun jumped in his fist, and the bullet caught the deputy dead-center in the forehead. A pebbly clot of brain matter erupted from the back of his skull and sprayed the back-bar mirror. The would-be murderer folded dead over the bar before the corpse slid to the floor.

When the smoke cleared, the stink of saltpeter mixed with the sweet, coppery smell of blood.

"Jesus Christ with a wooden dick!" one of the cow nurses exclaimed. "Did you *see* that shot, boys?"

A delighted Booger slammed the table with a fist as solid as a cedar mallet. "Hell, I ain't had this much fun since the hogs ate Maw-maw! Fargo the Trailsman is back!"

"Could this be love?" Fargo said sarcastically as he unfolded to his feet and leathered his shooter.

"You all right?" McDade said.

"I'll have to dig some buckshot outta my leg when we get back," Fargo replied. "But it's a long way from my heart."

"Fargo," Deke admired, "you got the nervous system of an oyster. Man alive! The Skinny Wolf musta promised that crooked deputy plenty of money for killing you."

"Ladies," Fargo addressed the soiled doves, "I don't know which one of you warned me, but I'm sure beholden. Trouble is, I just killed a deputy in a Texas town. 'Self-defense' won't cut much ice around here."

"Long-tall, you've got it all wrong," a buxom redhead wearing an ostrich-feather boa assured him. "A Mexican just waltzed in here and gunned Pete down in cold blood, ain't that right, girls?"

"Right as rain," answered a blonde with a garishly painted face. "A big, mean Mexican with a pox-scarred face. Besides, Sheriff Waldo rode out this afternoon to serve a warrant over in Puma Springs, and he won't be back before midnight."

"As for us," one of the cowboys said, "we weren't even here tonight."

And ten seconds later they weren't.

Fargo had been prepared to spend twenty dollars earlier to find out if that whiskey was poisoned. Before he and his companions forked leather, he gave it to the women. Deke added five for the undertaker.

"Boys," Fargo said after they'd pointed their bridles back toward camp, "we jumped over a snake tonight—two snakes, actually. But I know El Lobo—somehow he found out Quintana is hauling a fortune in that coach, and he's determined to get it come hell or high water."

"I think we got other problems, too," Deke said. "Problems closer to home, if you take my drift?"

"I take it," Fargo assured him, eyes scouring the moon-bleached terrain. "Old man Quintana is a sly old bird, all right, and something ain't jake about these Spaniards with him. I can't puzzle it out yet, but we have to find out without tipping our hand."

"Maybe they're planning a big heist," McDade suggested. "Or maybe they already pulled one—it's not just Booger weighting that coach down."

"I'd say that's not too likely," Fargo replied. "There's too many of them and they don't act like men on the dodge. Besides, most of Quintana's story about his past is true—I got it from a colonel at Fort Smith who knows him and said he's wealthy."

"*All* of you shut your fish traps!" Booger snarled, rolling side to side on Ambrose as the ox lumbered along. "T'hell with Skinny Wolf and the garlics—old Booger got no pussy tonight, and it's still a long haul to San Antone. But you can bet your bucket the catfish here will get a stinky finger any damn time he wants it, the piker!"

"From your lips to God's ears," Fargo retorted. "But there's more than one way to pump a woman. I got a hunch Katrina Robles might know something we don't, and the first chance I get I'm gonna try to find out."

11

Fargo's plan to get Katrina Robles aside and question her ran into unexpected difficulties.

Evidently Viceroy Hernando Quintana now harbored suspicions about the two women—or more likely, about his womanizing scout. They were still allowed the luxury of a hot bath every other night, and the old man still gave them their privacy by joining his men around their separate campfire.

But now a walking sentry circled the tent on bath nights, and Fargo couldn't risk trying to elude him. And every chance he did get to speak with either of the women, Quintana or Salazar was within earshot.

"The old man is nervous," Fargo told Booger and Cherokee Bob. "I'd say he suspects we're starting to snap wise to the fact that he's up to something besides traveling west for his health."

It was late afternoon on day nineteen of the California journey, one week exactly since Fargo's double brush with death back in Victoria. Earlier that day they had wisely bypassed San Antonio, the last place Quintana and his men wanted to pass through in force.

The Alamo battle had been fought and lost twenty-five years earlier, but feelings still ran high and Texans were not all that disposed to distinguish between Mexicans and Spaniards—especially Spaniards hauling along a cannon and artillery rifle. Booger had once again missed a chance to consort with sporting girls, and his foul mood lingered.

"Damn your red hide!" he snapped at All Behind Him. "Must you make such an infernal racket when you eat?"

The perpetually hungry Delaware had managed to filch a bag of parched corn from a supply wagon. Now he sat grinding it up with his toothless, machine-press mouth, ignoring the conversation.

Booger moved upwind of the Delaware, wrinkling his moon face in disgust.

"Don't that glutton son of a bitch *never* take a bath? Christ, he stinks like a four-holer in the dog days."

"Fox smells his own hole first," Cherokee Bob replied.

Fargo and Booger had walked beyond the main camp to join the Indians in their own rustic camp. The terrain had changed dramatically during the past week. On his scouting loops earlier that day, Fargo was forced to slap at buffalo gnats while watching dusty coyotes slink away through jagged seams and gullies—all beneath a Western sky so blue and bottomless it roared inside a man's skull.

"Say, you Shawnee heathen." Booger addressed Cherokee Bob. "You palaver Espanish—the hell does *tonto* mean? Fargo knows but he won't tell me."

"It means 'stupid.'"

"Hell, is that all? I figured Rivera was insulting me. And speaking on things old Booger is too stupid to know . . . what's this 'crick-crack' foolishness Fargo warned me and the rest about?"

"Never mind that," Fargo cut in impatiently. "We didn't come out here to discuss the causes of the wind."

He looked at Cherokee Bob, who sat on a flat rock picking his teeth with a twig.

"I've tried to listen in on the Spaniards," Fargo said, "but I just can't pick up all that much. I can understand some Spanish, but it's like you said, Bob—these Spaniards don't use the lingo like Mexers do."

"I say we just kill all the men, divvy up the gold or silver, and screw both the women till they limp," Booger said. "I don't mind eating off Fargo's plate."

"I like fuck," All Behind Him agreed, corn falling from his mouth.

Fargo waved their foolishness aside.

"Have you heard anything suspicious at all?" he asked the Shawnee.

"You 'member last night how the wind was howling like mating wolves?"

Fargo nodded. A fierce wind had polished the knolls bare and turned sand and grit into buckshot.

"Well, there was two men in a picket post priddy near where me and Toothless here holed up. Now and again the wind would blow in a snatch of their talk just as clear as if they was right beside us. Twice I heard one of them say '*los otros al Benicia*—the others at Benicia.' You ever heard of a place by that name?"

Fargo started to shake his head no. Then suddenly he alerted like a hound on point.

"You sure that's what you heard—Benicia?"

"Sounded like it."

"So what?" Booger said. "What's Benicia?"

"There's a naval armory by that name in California," Fargo replied, slowly pondering this new information. "The *only* military armory in California, matter of fact. Small arms, black powder, pig lead, and bullet moulds, a few bigger guns, mortars, and such."

"That don't make no sense," Booger scoffed. "A naval armory? You ain't saying these dagos—"

"I'm not saying a damn thing except there's a naval armory by that name in the very state we're headed to. Hell, maybe they're talking about a place by that name in Spain."

"The armory," Cherokee Bob said. "Huh. It must be well guarded."

"There's a small contingent of American marines there. Maybe fifty or so last I heard of it. Not a big force, but marines are tough scrappers and excellent marksmen. And it's on a little island, not an easy place to seize."

"It would take a lot bigger force than this bunch," Cherokee Bob opined, "to whip them marines. And they're in a battle fortification, right?"

Fargo nodded. "Even those two guns Quintana's hauling would be next to useless."

"Both you two are jackasses," Booger scoffed. "This bunch is pee doodles. The hell you tryin' to say—that they're fixin' to take California back for Spain? Eighteen garlics led by an old man? Christmas crackers!"

"You're forgetting *los otros*," Fargo pointed out. "The others. What if there's a bunch out there waiting to join them?"

"A bunch," Cherokee Bob added, "just waiting on the money Quintana is hauling in that coach."

Booger snorted. "Hookey Walker! You don't just waltz in—"

"I didn't say anything like that is going on," Fargo snapped. "But they always talk who never think. You don't know one damn thing about California. You've never been there, but I have plenty of times. The idea's not as far-fetched as you think. There's damn little law in California and even less military."

"Fargo's right," Cherokee Bob pitched in. "I been there, too. What passes for law in San Francisco is a bunch of criminal, vigilante trash who call themselves the Hounds. They'll serve any master who tosses them a few crumbs from the table."

Fargo nodded. "There's another problem—this War Between the States that's just brewing up back east. Most are saying it'll be over in a few months at most, but I think it's gonna drag on."

By now Booger looked thoughtful. "Aye, and mayhap old man Quintana thinks the same thing—even *counts* on it."

"If this war does drag on," Fargo said, "there'll be no soldiers to spare for California. And even if some were sent, by the time they got there, a new government could have the few fortifications manned."

"It's no skin off my Indian ass," Cherokee Bob said. "Everybody shits on the red man. But I druther deal with the Devil I know—these damn Spaniards are too keen to kill in the name of their God."

"Well, it's all air pudding right now," Fargo said. "No point in stacking our conclusions higher than our evidence— we need more information. C'mon, Booger, let's get back to camp. I smell Deke's cooking, and maybe I can get a word in with Katrina."

"Hold up a minute, Fargo," Cherokee Bob said.

Looking solemn, he pulled a small fox-fur pouch out from behind his shirt. "You 'member the watch I won off that barge man in St. Louis?"

"I do," Fargo said. "He had a straight open at both ends and couldn't fill it."

"Yeah, him. Anyhow, I figure if anybody survives this

trip, it's likely to be you. I want you to hold this. Case I'm killed, make sure it gets a good home. This ain't no ord'nary timepiece."

Lovingly, Cherokee Bob extracted an unimpressive pocket watch from the pouch and gazed upon it.

"Looks like a cheap watch to me," Booger scoffed.

"Likely it is cheap. But its value ain't in the watch—it's who owned it."

Booger studied it more closely. "How's 'at? Who owned it?"

"Read the inscription on the back of the case," Cherokee Bob said, carefully handing the watch over.

Booger had very little schooling. He squinted, lips slowly sounding out the words. "'To Daniel with all my love, Betty.'"

He looked at the Shawnee. "So what, Catfish? It musta been a piddling bet if you took this in payment."

"Piddling, huh? The fellow I won it from was named Boone."

"You mean . . . ah, serve it on toast, you lying sack of shit. Old Booger ain't falling for no more of your swindles. This was never Dan'l Boone's watch."

"So you don't believe me?"

"Does a fat baby fart?"

"My hand to God it's true, McTeague. I won it from Daniel Boone's grandson, Peyton. See, Boone's wife, Betty, gave it to him before Daniel went off on one of his long hunts."

"Do you see any green on my antlers?" Booger scoffed.

"Ask Fargo, you big blowhard. He was in the same poker game when I won it."

Booger turned to Fargo. "Is that straight-arrow, Skye? Was you there when Chief Blanket Ass won this watch?"

"I was," Fargo replied truthfully. "Bob cheated, but he won it. No misdoubting that."

Booger read the inscription again. "Well, I'm clemmed! Wouldja sell it?"

Cherokee Bob shook his head. "Nope. This watch is a piece of history."

"The hell do you care about white man's history? You just got done whining 'bout how everybody shits on the red man. 'Sides, Dan'l Boone was an Injun killer and sent plenty from your tribe to their scaffolds."

"Don't matter. He's a famous man."

"I'll give you three dollars right now, cash on the barrelhead."

"Go suck your mother's dug."

"Five dollars," Booger said.

"I can't—"

"*Ten* dollars," Booger said. "That's my final offer, John."

Cherokee Bob rubbed his chin, studying the watch. "Well, it's worth a heap more than that. But I'm so broke I can't even pay attention. I'll let it go for ten and regret it the rest of my life."

Booger hastily dug a gold shiner from his chamois money pouch. The moment Cherokee Bob accepted the money, Booger howled in triumph.

"Well, I *guess* it's worth a heap more, you ignut savage! This watch will make old Booger a rich man. That'll learn you to bargain with your betters."

Cherokee Bob locked glances with Fargo, who was forced to bite his lower lip hard to keep a straight face.

"Yeah," Cherokee Bob replied. "Looks like you porked me good this time."

After supper that evening Fargo finally managed to draw Katrina Robles off from the others for a few minutes in the shadow of the chuck wagon.

"Looks like we won't be meeting in the tent again, pretty lady," he said. "Once was nice but not enough—for me, anyway."

"Nor I. Miranda, too, deeply resents her father's increased vigilance."

Fargo glanced around in the gathering twilight. There was no time for the subtle approach.

"Yeah, well, about her father . . . what's he *really* up to, Katrina?"

"I am a woman, Skye."

He grinned. "Yeah, I've noticed."

"What I mean is that he does not confide in me or Miranda. I am, after all, only a paid servant."

"Servants see and hear plenty. F'rinstance, is Quintana really heading west because of his health?"

Her eyes fled from his and she took a deep breath to fortify herself.

"I will tell you this much, Skye, and no more, for I am afraid of *all* of these men. Hernando Quintana smiles kindly and speaks with diplomatic civility. But like Salazar, Aragon, and that two-legged pig Rivera, there is only a lump of sod where his heart should be. Be careful, for they are all brutal men."

"Senorita Robles!"

"Fade," Fargo told her, watching the unholy trinity hurrying toward the couple. "I'll handle this."

Booger, seeing what was unfolding, deserted his coffee and moved closer.

"Fargo," Salazar greeted him, "the entire world knows that you are a randy stallion. But sate your desires on the whores—our women are not for your pleasure."

"That's up to them," Fargo said, "not you."

Salazar's straight-as-a-seam mouth compressed itself even tighter.

"*Them?* Do you include Miranda in this unwise boast?"

"Since there's only two women with us," Fargo retorted, "I'd say you have a remarkable grasp for the obvious. And it's not a boast—it's a fact. With me, it's always the lady's choice."

Salazar's breathing quickened until Fargo could hear it faintly whistling in his nostrils. "And are you telling me Miranda has already succumbed?"

"Of course not," Fargo lied. "Nor has Katrina."

"You are surrounded on all sides, Fargo, day and night. Do not turn your tongue into a shovel and bury yourself with it."

"No need," Fargo told him, "to take the long way around the barn, *comprende?* If you're threatening to kill me, spell it out plain like a man."

Fargo's hand was now poised over his holster. That realization suddenly brought Salazar to Jesus. His tone grew more reasonable.

"I was speaking metaphorically, of course."

Rivera, however, could not restrain his contempt and rage. "*Capitan, con respeto* . . . with all due respect, do not let this pagan infidel intimidate you! He needs to understand who his betters are."

"Well, if it ain't Sergeant Rivera," Fargo goaded, shifting

his gaze to the brute. "Living proof that you can breed a jackass and a pig. Just curious: You been leaving any more notes for El Lobo?"

Even in the fading light, Rivera's eyes were luminous with insanity. He snarled like a rabid animal and started to snatch the machete from its scabbard.

But Fargo had deliberately goaded him to this, believing that in unknown waters it was sometimes better to rock the boat than submit to the rudder. Moving swift as a striking snake, he lifted his right foot up and tugged the Arkansas toothpick from its boot sheath.

Rivera had just cleared the scabbard when Fargo drove two inches of solid cast iron into the meaty portion of the tyrant's left thigh. Rivera howled in pain and dropped the machete.

Fargo was not, however, quite finished. An Arkansas toothpick was fashioned as both knife and club, and at the base of the haft was a knob of solid iron. Fargo yanked the blade from Rivera's thigh, deftly spun the weapon around, and drove the knob up hard under Rivera's chin.

There was a noise like dice clacking as Rivera's upper and lower teeth smashed together hard. Then his knees came unhinged and he flopped to the ground, alone with the music of the Spheres.

All this happened in mere seconds. Lieutenant Juan Aragon recovered from his surprise and tore at the sidearm in his flap holster.

There was a loud, flat metallic *click* when Booger cocked the hammer of his huge Colt's Dragoon pistol.

"Try it, pepper-gut, and you'll be shoveling coal in hell."

Rivera's howl of pain had brought Hernando Quintana at a run.

"Senor Fargo! I did not hire you to brawl with my men and leave them within an inch of their lives."

Fargo sheathed the toothpick. "He's damn lucky he's still got an inch. I had every right to sink that blade in his heart. He pulled that machete on me, and in Texas that's murderous intent. The next time that swine looks at me cross-eyed, I *will* kill him."

Quintana loosed a long sigh. "Clearly tensions are rising

dangerously. We have all been under a strain. Senor Fargo, I was saving this as a surprise for you and your companions. I have already made arrangements to lodge everyone on this expedition—except the Indians, of course—at the Montezuma House when we reach Las Cruces in New Mexico Territory, at my expense. We will all rest in luxury for three days. Perhaps a welcome break will ease the tensions."

This news surprised Fargo. With the exception of the Patee House in St. Joseph, there was no finer hotel in the American West than the Montezuma House.

"That's mighty generous of you, don Hernando."

Quintana looked at Salazar. "Diego, as officer in charge, you must make Sergeant Rivera understand—we are not common murderers. And we need Fargo. Have you already forgotten that hair-raising incident with the wild longhorns? Miranda might have been killed if not for his and Mr. McTeague's quick actions."

"But, don Hernando, Fargo deliberately provoked Sergeant—"

"*Basta!* If you cannot get along with this man, stay away from him. I have watched him, and he is not one to seek trouble."

Quintana turned and stalked away, clearly angry. Rivera, awash on a sea of pain, groaned piteously and tried to sit up.

Booger squatted on his heels beside him. "Who's your pappy *now*, Coronado, huh?"

"Sew up your lips, you tangle-brained fool," Fargo muttered. "The man's been whipped. No need for hot-jawing now."

The two men headed toward the rope corral.

"Fargo, you son of trouble, old Booger is proud of you."

"Does this mean I'm spoken for?"

He didn't share Booger's elation. On the western frontier, the end of one fight usually marked the beginning of the next, and the words that had pestered Fargo at the outset of this expedition returned now in full force:

"Wait for what will come. . . ."

12

Things went bad for Booger the next morning, even before he'd finished his breakfast. His first mishap was a matter of unfortunate timing.

Ever since acquiring the "Daniel Boone" watch from Cherokee Bob the day before, Booger had been scheming about making a huge profit from it. Fargo, averting his face to hide a grin, watched his friend set his plate aside and pull the watch from his pocket. He fixed his eye on Bitch Creek McDade, who was known to be flush with cash.

"C'mere, Bitch," he called out.

Unfortunately for Booger, Miranda Quintana had started to return to her tent and was only a few feet in front of Booger when he spoke.

Her pretty face flushed scarlet, and she slapped Booger so hard his floppy hat flew off. "How dare you insult me, you . . . you behemoth barbarian!"

Fargo, McDade, and Deke burst into laughter.

"I meant the *other* Bitch, Muffin," Booger explained, a red handprint glowing on his cheek.

"He wasn't insulting you, Miss Quintana," McDade volunteered. "That word he just used really is my front name."

"Mr. McDade, I find you to be a pleasant and well-mannered man. Please do not tell lies to cover for this . . . this fat oaf!"

"Fat, is it?" Booger said. "And have you ever stopped to consider that if everyone in the world was fat, we'd all be closer together?"

Miranda scowled petulantly and answered with a sarcastic rhyme. "'You beat your pate, and fancy wit will come; knock as you please, there's nobody home.'"

"No, Miss Quintana, it's true," McDade insisted. "I was

born in a little hamlet called Bitch Creek, Tennessee, and my father decided he liked the name."

"And your mother didn't object?"

"She did, but she just took to calling me Mickey."

Miranda turned to Booger. "I apologize, Mr. McTeague. And you're not fat—you're just big."

Diego Salazar, who had taken to watching over Miranda like a miser over his gold, spoke up.

"Do not apologize to peasant stock, Miranda. McTeague, you will not use that word in front of her again."

Miranda's mischievous eyes sought out Fargo. "Oh, I'm not so delicate and proper as all that, Captain Salazar."

"These base and vulgar men are corrupting you. You must remember—"

Booger cut him off. "Get over your peeve, poncy-man. You seen what Rivera got last night from a base and vulgar man. There's plenty more where that come from."

Salazar, perhaps remembering the viceroy's order to avoid trouble, spun neatly on his heel and left to ready his men for the trail. Fargo watched Booger collar Deke and McDade.

"Boys," he announced grandly, "I have something here that could fetch either one of you a tidy little pile of wampum. That ignorant Shawnee let it slip through his fingers."

"Looks like a four-bit watch to me," Deke said. "Look—the face is cracked."

"Ah? A four-bit watch is it? Ha-ho, ha-ho! Read the inscription."

"'To Daniel with all my love, Betty.'"

Deke shrugged. "If you wander near a point, don't be afraid to make it."

"The *point*, you two-legged cabinet, is that this here very watch was give to Dan'l Boone by his loving wife, Betty. An angelic soul, she was."

Deke laughed so hard he had to drop to one knee. "Booger, you consarn fool! Daniel Boone's wife was named Becky—Rebecca Boone. That conniving Injun has rooked you agin."

Booger looked like a man who had wakened on the ceiling. Suddenly his face purpled with rage.

"Fargo, you son of a motherless goat! You said you was

there when that treacherous savage won this from Dan'l's grandson, Peyton Boone."

"Now hold your powder. You asked me if I was there when he won the watch. I never said the jasper he won it from was named Peyton Boone."

"Is this what the white man has sunk to—standing by idle while a low-down, skunk-bit Shawnee skins another white man out of ten dollars? I will—"

Abruptly the wolf howl of alarm sounded from the Indians' camp nearby.

"Trouble's on the spit," Fargo told Booger, snatching up his Henry. "C'mon."

Fargo stopped by his saddle long enough to grab his binoculars. As soon as he cleared the main camp, he saw it on the western horizon: a yellow-brown dust plume.

"Looks like Comanches," he said grimly. "They ride in echelon, and that plume is wide."

Booger spat. "Comanches? Well, I'm glad for it! No placid punkin butter life for old Booger."

Despite Booger's predictable bravado, however, Fargo had enough sense to worry. There was a good chance the Comanches' battle cousins, the Kiowas, would be riding with them. Of all the great horse tribes beyond the hundredth meridian—the "blood meridian"—Fargo most feared the Comanche and Kiowa tribes.

While their fighting skills and courage were no greater than those of the warrior tribes to the north, they far surpassed them in sheer ruthlessness and bloodlust.

"How many you make it to be?" Cherokee Bob greeted Fargo. "Judging from the plume, I'd say maybe three or four clans."

Fargo focused his spyglass and made a careful study. "Maybe seventy-five or eighty. This ain't no renegade band tossed together for a quick raid. I see the shields of the Sash Warriors riding alongside the Comanch."

"Sash Warriors? What's them?" Booger demanded.

"Kaitsenko," Cherokee Bob said. "Kiowa warrior society. Once they don their red sashes and close for the attack, there's no retreat allowed. They have to kill or be killed."

"They know we're here," Fargo said, "and they'll be on us

in half an hour or so. Think you might know their battle chief?"

"If he ain't been killed, there's a good chance it's the Comanche Iron Eyes of the Antelope Eater Clan."

"I recall the name."

"You should. He controls this stretch west of San Antone. He knows me, all right. I worked out a deal one time, put him on to some stolen Army Spencers. He hates the Crow tribe to the north, and he knows it was a Crow bit my ear off, so he tolerates me."

"Think he'll parley if we set up a pole?"

"He might listen to us," Cherokee Bob replied. "And if them damn Sash Warriors wasn't along with him, we might wangle out of a fight. But he'll be showing off for the Kiowas."

"Let's at least make it look like we're trying the peace road first," Fargo decided. "We need to halt them if we can."

Diego Salazar, walking ramrod straight and accompanied by Hernando Quintana and Lieutenant Juan Aragon, approached them from the camp.

"Where's the gimlet-eyed pig?" Cherokee Bob said.

"You might say Sergeant Rivera is feeling poorly this morning," Booger replied. "He's got him a bad case of whipping cough. By the bye, you Shawnee shit, after this little barn dance, you and me has got a bone to pick."

"What is the trouble, Senor Fargo?" Quintana asked, hurrying closer—moving quite nimbly, Fargo noticed, for an old man supposedly stricken with health problems.

Fargo quickly explained the situation and his advice for handling it.

"This is a military matter, don Hernando," Captain Salazar insisted officiously. "I will take command. We will set the cannon and artillery rifle on that low rise in front of us with the men in fighting holes just behind the ridge where the savages cannot easily see them. As soon as they are in effective range, we will open fire."

Quintana considered this, then looked at Fargo. "And you say . . . ?"

"The captain's got it right, don Hernando, on where to place the men and guns. But he's confusing Southern Plains warriors with European armies and set-piece battles."

"You question my military training?" Salazar demanded.

Actually Fargo did, but this was no time to be measuring dicks.

"No. I reckon it's fine for fighting Napoleon. But these Comanches and Kiowas aren't stupid—they won't come to us in a full frontal assault once you open fire on them. They'll just swing around us on the flanks at the first shots and head right for the camp—they aren't here to die gloriously. They're raiders and plunderers."

"And you," Salazar said, "believe you can *talk* these heathen marauders out of attacking?"

"Not likely. But Cherokee Bob thinks they'll at least listen to us first—all Indians are naturally curious. That means they'll stop and congregate in one spot. Then, when the talk breaks down, you'll have targets. You'll have to hit them hard and fast and keep your men out of sight as long as you can. It's our only chance against a force this big."

Quintana said, "It makes sense to me, Diego. Fargo knows this enemy."

Salazar surprised Fargo by nodding agreement. He turned to Aragon.

"Lieutenant," he snapped crisply, "put Raoul and Alejandro on the big guns. Form the men up with their entrenching tools and have them dig in at five-yard intervals. *De prisa!* Hurry!"

Booger snickered when Aragon actually saluted. Fargo, however, wondered what kind of informal "militia" made up of sugarcane harvesters came equipped with entrenching tools.

"Don Hernando," Fargo said, "I take it you have a firearm?"

The viceroy looked startled. "Of course. You wish me to join the battle?"

Fargo shook his head. "No. You'll have a more important job. You need to go back and stay in the tent with Miranda and Katrina."

"Well, I am no soldier. But certainly I will do my best to protect—"

"That's not what I mean. If this battle goes bad for us and those savages take the camp, you do *not* want women falling into the hands of Kiowas and Comanches."

Quintana paled. "You don't mean . . . ?"

"That's exactly what I mean. Killing them will be merciful compared to the alternative. And make sure there's a third bullet for yourself."

Fargo quickly returned to the main camp and tacked the Ovaro before returning to the Indians' camp. Deke Lafferty and Bitch Creek McDade came out to join Fargo and his companions. Both men nervously watched the boiling, yellow-brown dust cloud move inexorably closer and closer.

"Trailsman, can I take a squint through the spyglass?" Deke asked.

Fargo handed them over.

"Lord," Deke said after a few moments of study, "it does give the heart a jump, don't it? Their faces is painted in green and yellow stripes like African witch doctors'."

"Battle colors," Fargo said. "They don't paint because they think it's powerful medicine like a Sioux or Cheyenne does. They just know it scares the crap outta their enemies."

From the main camp came the shouted command *"Adelante!"*

Fargo watched Aragon quick-march the fifteen "plantation workers."

"I'll be damned," Cherokee Bob said. "All of 'em in perfect step."

"At least they can drill," Fargo agreed.

"Fuerza . . . alta!" Aragon barked, halting the men. *"Orden . . . armas!"*

The men crisply brought their Volcanic rifles to order arms.

"Hazlo!" he snapped, and they grounded their weapons, using their spade-bladed entrenching tools to dig rifle pits.

"Fargo, those look like soldiers, sure enough," Cherokee Bob said. "I wonder if they shoot as good as they march."

"Let's hope so. Those Volcanic repeaters don't have much stopping power, but the magazine holds thirty rounds."

Fargo nodded toward the gun wagon, now parked in place near the line of Spanish troops.

"Pretty quick now, you two get out of sight behind that wagon," he told Deke and McDade. "You, too, Booger."

"Teach your grandmother to suck eggs," Booger shot back. "Old Booger is riding out with you and the Injins."

"Forget it. That ox of yours is too slow and we'll be beating a hasty retreat. They'll shoot you to rag tatters and eat Ambrose."

Cherokee Bob peered through the glasses. "I was right. It's Iron Eyes leading them. I recognize his scalp cape."

The rolling thunder grew louder as the attackers continued to pound their steeds across the arid landscape. Fargo had borrowed Salazar's saber as a parley pole, tying his red bandanna to the hilt and jabbing the weapon point first into the ground about a hundred yards out ahead.

Booger's bravado was wearing a little thin.

"Fargo, where is your mind? Them red sons ain't likely to parley—look at 'em! Bouncing up and down on them scrubs and actin' crazier'n dogs in the hot moons."

"Looks like they got liquor from the Comancheros," Fargo surmised.

"'R mebbe et peyote," Deke said. "C'mon, Bitch, we ain't no Indian fighters. Let's get hid 'fore they swarm us. They're headed for us straight as a plumb line."

"Catfish, if you figure you can just ride out and talk to *this* bunch," Booger insisted, "you're putting your thumb on the scale. They'll fill you and them flea-bit redskins so fulla arrahs you'll look like porky-pines."

"Hell, I don't plan to live forever," Fargo replied. "Anyhow, we have to make them halt or they'll break for the camp. Just get behind that gun wagon and make your North and Savage sing when the time comes to open the ball. Let's make tracks, boys!"

Fargo slapped the Ovaro's rump. A minute later the three men halted their mounts, Fargo on one side of the parley pole, the Shawnee and Delaware on the other.

Cherokee Bob had to raise his voice to be heard above the rataplan of rapidly approaching hooves.

"Christ, Fargo, I hope them sons of de Soto behind us can shoot straight. We're smack dab between them and Iron Eyes's bunch."

"Cheer up," Fargo said. "We'll likely never survive the Coman—"

Fargo halted midsentence, staring in disbelief at All Behind Him. The Delaware calmly sat his mule, shoving handfuls of parched corn from a hide sack into his rock-crusher mouth. He saw Fargo staring.

"No like die hungry," he explained.

Cherokee Bob grinned proudly. "Ain't he a pip?"

He was forced to shout now because the wave of war-greased Kiowas and Comanches was about to engulf them. Despite Fargo's calm exterior, he could feel his heartbeat throbbing in his palms. These next few seconds would determine whether he lived or died. All tribes were highly notional, even more so when they were liquored.

The mules stood calmly, but the Ovaro wanted to break and run, and Fargo couldn't blame him. He patted the side of the stallion's neck, but couldn't keep him from repeatedly rearing.

Closer, ever closer, so close now that Fargo could see the hard metallic eyes that had earned the Comanche war chief his name. The Comanche ponies ran strong, their uncut tails streaming out behind them and so long they would touch the ground at a standstill. Red human hands painted on the horses' hips symbolized the riders' battle kills.

Fargo had trained the Ovaro to hate the smell of bear grease, which many Indian braves smeared through their hair. Now Fargo had all he could do to control his stallion. Just when it seemed the raiding party must overrun the three men flanking the parley pole, Iron Eyes thrust his red-streamered lance into the air and the Indians halted their mounts in a choking cloud of dust.

Most Comanches spoke some Spanish and English, necessary in their dealings with traders, gunrunners, and others in Mexico and the United States.

"Cherokee Bob," Iron Eyes greeted the Shawnee. "Now you play the dog for your new *gauchupine* masters?"

"The food is damn good, Iron Eyes. It was Fargo who hired me, not the *gauchupines*."

The Comanche's lips curled back off his teeth in contempt. His eyes shifted to Fargo. "So this is the great hunter, scout, and Indian killer whose fame stretches from here to the place where the sun rests? Fargo, you have killed many Comanches, uh?"

Fargo feigned boredom. Comanches, like most braves, despised fear or shows of respect from their enemies.

"Kill one fly, kill a million," he replied.

Iron Eyes grunted. "El Lobo Flaco will pay me in whiskey and guns for your severed head. Perhaps you will pay even more to keep it on your shoulders."

Fargo noted that the Kiowa Sash Warriors, five of them, rode directly to Iron Eyes's right in the place of honor. He resolved to kill all of them first. He had to because once the fandango started, only death would stop them—and he would be their first target. The brave who killed Skye Fargo would be sung about for generations to come.

"What kind of pay do you ask?" Cherokee Bob said. "We're here to talk terms."

"Good fire sticks made in the land of the beefeaters. Powder and lead. Whiskey. Mules to eat."

Fargo shook his head. "You can have a few mules. Food, coffee, sugar. But no weapons and no whiskey."

Iron Eyes glanced quickly toward the Sash Warriors, then again at Fargo. His eyes glowed with murderous rage. "Fargo, would you put the shawl on me while my braves look on?"

As he said this, the Comanche leader glanced past Fargo to the gun wagons. His evident curiosity told Fargo he knew little or nothing about those two big guns.

"No weapons or whiskey," Fargo repeated, knowing full well that Iron Eyes had no intention of bargaining in good faith—he intended to sack the camp and would settle for nothing less. He was simply buying time while he sized up the situation and nerved up for the command.

"Have ears for my words, hair face. Perhaps I will kill the white legend and his Shawnee dog now."

"Bad idea, Iron Eyes," Cherokee Bob said. "Let's all be friends, huh? I've got some good tobacco. Let's smoke a pipe to the four directions."

Iron Eyes ignored this. "I see two *gauchupine* soldiers behind you. El Lobo said there are more."

Now Fargo realized the "Red Raiders of the Plains" had not spotted the men in the rifle pits.

"They're protecting the main camp," Fargo lied.

Again Iron Eyes glanced toward the Sash Warriors, a glance that seemed to be a signal. Fargo caught Cherokee Bob's eyes and nodded.

"Crick," the Shawnee said quietly.

"Crack," All Behind Him responded.

Fargo's heart sat out the next few beats. *The readiness is all,* he reminded himself.

Cherokee Bob fired his big hand cannon from behind his tatty corduroy jacket, smoke and flame and burning cloth belching just ahead of a crack-booming roar that instantly panicked many of the Comanche horses.

A fist-sized hole was punched through Iron Eyes's bone breastplate, chunks of flesh, organs, and shattered spine spraying out behind him. The roaring detonation was still ringing in Fargo's ears when All Behind Him flipped his moth-eaten blanket aside and opened up at near point-blank range with his Manhattan Arms pepperbox. In a blur of speed he fired, rotated the next barrel in place, fired again.

At the same time Fargo's Colt seemed to leap into his fist and he fanned the hammer, rapidly killing or wounding the deadly Sash Warriors with lightning speed. All three defenders had opened up so quickly that not one enemy brave had fired back before the six-pounder boomed behind Fargo.

The exploding ball struck on the left end of the skirmish line, launching two screaming braves skyward on a plume of fire and dirt. The Parrot artillery rifle added to the mayhem, each whistling shell killing or wounding men and horses.

Not even ten seconds had passed before the scene was absolute bedlam. But the coup de main came when, with a collective battle cry, the Spanish soldiers opened up with their Volcanic rifles. It sounded as if a giant ice floe were slowly cracking apart as they emptied their thirty-shot magazines into the panicked and retreating enemy.

Fargo didn't even bother to break out his Henry. The withering fire made him and his two Indian companions cringe with the expectation of getting killed in the lead bath. But the highly disciplined and skillful marksmen held tight beads. Incredibly, when Salazar shouted the cease-fire command less than a minute later, the surviving renegades were fleeing to the west having never fired a bullet or nocked an arrow.

The ground in front of Fargo was littered with dead and dying braves and their horses, more than one-third of the force. Gray-white smoke hazed the battlefield, and the acrid stench of spent powder mingled with the sweet tang of blood.

Fargo met Cherokee Bob's eyes, then gigged the Ovaro closer to his position.

"Benicia." Bob greeted him. "It's *got* to be the naval armory they're after. These Spanish devils mean to take over California, Fargo. *Damn* but they are fearsome."

Fargo watched as the soldiers fanned out and tossed finishing shots into the wounded.

"Sure looks that way," Fargo agreed. "But good as they are, they won't take that marine garrison."

"Not by themselves. But you're forgetting about *los otros*."

"Yeah. The others."

Fargo watched Booger emerge from behind the gun wagon carrying his North & Savage. The Trailsman doubted that he had even gotten off a shot. He appeared to be shocked speechless by what he had just witnessed—a rare condition for Booger.

"Hey, McTeague," Cherokee Bob called out, "you said you got a bone to pick with me?"

"I was mighty mistaken, Catfish," Booger replied. "If I was stupid enough to think Daniel Boone's wife was named Betty, there's others I can slicker with that watch."

For a moment Fargo's eyes met Salazar's. The Spanish officer sent him a smug stare before he turned away.

"Bob," Fargo said quietly, "we are in a world of shit."

13

During the next fifteen days, the Quintana party, now traveling the old San Antonio Road, made excellent progress.

Terrain was mostly flat or only slightly hilly across the vast Edwards and Stockton plateaus, although they now faced increasing heat and stretches of water scarcity. More and more Fargo was forced to search out potable water, and at times he imposed rationing.

The Guadalupe Mountains, east of El Paso, would pose their first real brush with steeper terrain, but Fargo knew the trail was well routed through good passes.

Food supplies were still plentiful, but the diet was growing more monotonous as some staples gave out.

"I hope we spot a buff herd that's gone too far south," Deke said wistfully at suppertime one evening. "Hump steak cooked in kidney fat, and hot biscuits dripped in the pot liquor—you can't beat fixin's like that."

Fargo heartily agreed, but like the others he settled for salt junk and pemmican, supplemented occasionally with rabbit, antelope, or quail.

More important, to Fargo, was the lack of any additional Indian attacks. Word of the astonishing defeat of Iron Eyes and his warriors, just west of San Antonio, must have spread like a grass fire across the rest of Texas because there was no more trouble from renegade raiders.

"Is the serious Indian threat behind us now?" Hernando Quintana asked Fargo one morning as the Trailsman prepared to ride out on the day's first scout.

By now Fargo was far more worried about the nefarious treachery planned by the viceroy and these efficient killers traveling with him. But he opted for discretion and kept that thought to himself.

"I gave up trying to predict Indian thinking a long time ago," Fargo replied. "It's like trying to write your name on water. They know we're here, all right. But there's better than even odds we're safe until we get to the New Mexico Territory beyond El Paso."

"Apache country?"

Fargo nodded. "But they make forays into Old Mexico for months at a time. And when they're north of the Rio they tend to stay in the mountains and raid on the peaceful Pueblo villages. But if we catch their attention, they might probe us."

"Perhaps word has reached them about the San Antonio debacle."

"You can take that to the bank. The moccasin telegraph is as reliable as the white man's. But they already know all about the big-thundering guns, and unlike those Comanches and Kiowas, they won't go near them. They employ tactics learned from fighting white men, including long-range sniping. And they're experts at camouflage and concealment."

"Yes, and as the *federales* in Mexico have discovered, they are excellent marksmen."

"The best of all the free-ranging tribes," Fargo agreed. "They don't just count on big medicine to guide their bullets— they take careful aim and they know about adjusting sights and such. They don't worship horses, neither. Most would just as soon eat their mounts as ride them."

"Logically, then, wouldn't that make them less of a threat in open country?"

"Not hardly. By attacking on foot they've become expert at nighttime infiltration and silent killing. They use rawhide-wrapped rocks that kill just as sure as a bullet but silently."

"Senor Fargo, you certainly do know your enemies," Quintana said, watching Fargo closely for his reaction. That searching look seemed to say: *And have you guessed by now that your enemies surround you right here in camp?*

But Fargo kept his face deadpan and only replied casually, "It comes with the job, don Hernando."

After dark the four Americans had taken to congregating at the small outlying camp established every evening by

Cherokee Bob and All Behind Him. On the evening before the party was due to reach the Pecos River in west Texas, the six men had gathered as usual.

"Fargo," Bitch Creek McDade said, "I've been thinking. Do you believe Quintana intends to let us cut loose when this journey is over?"

"Why wouldn't he?" Booger interceded. "He figures we ain't got the mentality to twig his game."

"Booger, don't be a fool all your life," Fargo gainsaid. "He's craftier than you think, and he knows we suspect *some*thing. They won't likely make their move until we cross the desert and reach Fort Yuma. After that it's a straight shot across the Mojave to the San Bernardino Pass and down to the California coast. They're home free then."

"Wha'd'ya mean 'make their move'?" Deke demanded.

"I mean they'll kill all six of us, lunk-head."

"Why all six of us?" Cherokee Bob echoed. "Me and All Behind Him are just worthless flea-bit savages. No white man would listen to us if we tried to spin a tale about these devils."

"They'll kill you on principle for the reason Rivera said on the first day you joined the party—you got no souls."

"The hell do they think we walk on—the top of our feet?"

"Not *soles*, you idiot," Deke said. "*Souls*—your ticket to the white man's heaven."

"Speaking of Rivera," McDade said, "he doesn't swagger it around making the he-bear talk like he used to. But have you noticed how he watches you now, Fargo?"

Fargo had, indeed, noticed. Ever since the Trailsman had laid him out cold, the brutish sergeant was seething with white-hot hatred and the need for revenge.

"That skunk-bit curly wolf means to fix your flint, Fargo," Booger chimed in, "and he ain't par'tic'lar if the bullet is in the front or back."

"Yeah, but I been watching him close," Cherokee Bob said, "and I don't think he's leaving any more messages for the Skinny Wolf. I think that murdering son of a bitch and his gang gave it up as a bad job. We ain't seen hide nor hair of them in a coon's age."

"That's graveyard talk, Bob," Fargo warned. "It might

appear like he's given up, but I think he's just waiting for favoring terrain. I know how he thinks. Once he decides to pull a job, he hangs on like a tick. He wants that money like they want ice water in hell."

"Sure, Skye," Cherokee Bob argued, "but by now he knows how dangerous these Spaniards are. And he knows they're whatchacallits—fanatics loyal to the old man and to Spain. So he knows that killing you won't get him that swag, which we ain't never even seen, by the way."

"Well, far as killing me goes—he'll still try to snuff my wick because he hates me and knows I mean to kill him. And I'm telling you the truth about Ruth—he *won't* give up on that money. He'll watch and wait like a starving buzzard, looking for his chance."

"Skye," McDade said in a worried tone, "you and Booger have seen the elephant. This rough-and-tumble is old hat to you. But I've never been caught in a deal like this before. You say they'll likely kill all of us. So what are we going to do about it?"

"I'm still studying on that," Fargo admitted.

"Studying, is it?" Booger said. "Study a cat's tail! Hell's bells! We're all just scratching at fleas, and every day we're taking these yellow dogs closer to California. Let's just kill 'em. There's six of us—each man would only have to kill three apiece. See, we just name a time and day and then we all unlimber at once and commence to killing. Just like the Mormons done to them pilgrims at Mountain Meadows."

"Hell, that ain't such a bad plan," Cherokee Bob said.

"I've considered some version of that myself," Fargo admitted. "But there's problems with it. Deke's admitted he can't aim worth a damn, and neither him nor Bitch has ever shot a man before. Besides, we know now that these Spanish troops—and that's what they are—are all experienced killers. One little hitch, and all six of us will be getting our mail delivered by moles."

"Them Mormons at Mountain Meadows," Deke added, "was scattered in among the pilgrims they killed. At the signal, they only had to gun down whoever was right next to 'em. Ain't no way in hell we can get in 'mongst these garlics like that. 'Specially Cherokee Bob and that fat-assed eating machine over there."

"You cook good," All Behind Him mumbled. "But big mouth."

"We've got time to scratch out something better," Fargo said. "And before we go painting the landscape red, I'd like better proof. The clues are there, all right, but we need to make sure."

"Make sure you get some more pussy, you mean," Booger scoffed. "Well, if old man Quintana keeps his word, we will soon be living like rajahs at this fancy hotel in New Mexico. Damn your bones, Fargo, I *will* drain my snake in Las Cruces, and I will shoot any mother's son who tries to stop me."

At the same time Fargo and the rest were meeting, Hernando Quintana, Captain Salazar, Lieutenant Aragon, and Sergeant Rivera were conferring in the flickering shadows at the far edge of the trail camp.

"Gentlemen," Quintana said, his voice vibrant with impending triumph, "God himself has ordained the success of our mission. All of the pieces are lined up perfectly on the chessboard, and checkmate is but a few assured moves away."

The aging former viceroy paused to take a pinch of snuff.

"When we bypassed San Antonio," he resumed, "I sent Raoul into the city to bring back the newspapers. The news could not be better for us. Events are unfolding exactly as I had hoped. The papers are filled with ominous news—ominous for our enemies—about the war that will soon prostrate this nation. We will resurrect New Spain while these barbaric fools kill each other."

"And you will once again command a viceroyalty, don Hernando," Salazar said. "Only, this time, you will govern a rich district as vast as many entire nations."

"It is God's will, Diego, not mine. We are all instruments of the August Father above. And I am convinced the American federal government will lose this war and end up imprisoned. The Southern rebels, controlled by the plantation aristocracy, are at a fever pitch for war to protect their cotton markets, a source of immense wealth."

Juan Aragon said, "Your Excellency? If these Southern rebels do win, do you believe they might attempt to wrest California from us once we take her back?"

"I do not, Juan. You lived in the South—you know how they are. 'Cotton is King' is their motto, and in their obsession with this profitable commodity they value little else. Even California's fortune in gold has little appeal for them. So long as they retain their lucrative markets in England and Europe, they will have little desire for conflicts and entanglements beyond their own region."

"And perhaps," Salazar suggested, "New Spain could even become one of those markets. Nothing keeps the peace as effectively as profitable trade arrangements."

"*Preciso*. And unless they are fools, the Southern faction will also be preoccupied in making sure the Northern states cannot regain strength and overthrow their power. No, events in California will not stir their interest. Even if they were inclined to do so, the great distances involved make sending troops a great difficulty."

"I agree," Salazar said, "but they are fools to let this great gem of the Pacific slip through their fingers. Mining, forestry, fishing, agriculture . . . and with so many placid *indio* tribes living there, forced labor will guarantee fortunes for men who seize the opportunities."

"Men just like you, eh? Rest assured that all three of you—indeed, every man riding with us now—will reap the fruits."

"No greater reward, don Hernando, than the one you have already promised," Salazar reminded his superior.

"And do you think I would go back on that promise? Lead Spain to victory in California, Diego, and Miranda will be your wife and the mother of your babes."

"Pardon my frankness, Your Excellency. She is extremely strong-willed and independent. These are bad traits in a wife. Her . . . flirtations with a crude man like Fargo trouble me."

Quintana expelled a long sigh. "Yes, since her mother died she has not had the proper guidance. But where a father must surrender, a husband may impose his will."

"Don Hernando," Aragon spoke up, "I consider your plan for seizing *Californio* both brilliant and just. But will there be enough men waiting for us—enough, I mean, to seize Benicia and the other garrisons? The Americans will certainly fight."

"They will fight, Juan, yes. They are an ignorant people with no real history, but certainly they have courage. But Augustine Sandoval has quietly been enlisting loyalists and arranging for arms shipments. We are carrying enough silver *barras* to pay and equip them. California is militarily weak, and the American men there are undisciplined and poorly organized except for a few marines."

Rivera spoke up. *"Con permiso?"*

"Of course, Miguel, speak your mind! You, too, are a part of this historical undertaking."

"Don Hernando, Fargo and his companions—they suspect something."

"Claro. Fargo is too intelligent not to realize, by now, that we plan a military action of some sort."

Captain Salazar weighed in. "You were not there, Miguel, to see his face after the men slaughtered those heathen Comanches. Without question he suspects us."

"But will he really care?" Aragon said. "He refuses to take oaths to governments. A 'bunch quitter' is how Jerome Helzer described him back at Powder-horn."

"True enough," Quintana said. "But even a rustic loner like Fargo will draw the line at allowing a 'foreign power' to seize an American state. He may not swear allegiance to any flag, but he has never denied that he is an American."

"All due respect, don Hernando," Salazar said. "But though you are still a Spanish citizen, you are now officially an American, too."

Quintana chuckled. "Yes, a status I requested to allay suspicions. Which means my entire plan is treason, and if it fails I will die by hanging or firing squad. And which, in turn, also means we must kill all of the Americans with us."

"When, don Hernando?"

"Not too soon, Diego, unless it clearly becomes necessary. Fargo has proven very adept at his job, and so have the others. Speaking of Fargo . . ."

In the flickering burnt orange torchlight Quintana's seamed face swiveled toward Rivera.

"Miguel, what did Fargo mean by suggesting that you were leaving notes for this criminal, El Lobo Flaco?"

"A vile lie, don Hernando, intended to sew disharmony."

"Yes, quite possibly. I only ask because it does seem that someone among us may have informed him about the silver. At any rate, he seems to have moved on to other criminal enterprises."

"The massacre of so many savages," Salazar suggested, "has taught him the folly of trying to overcome our security."

"He may indeed have learned his lesson. But let me warn all of you: Fargo is a man who *teaches* lessons, hard lessons that often end in death. At the first sign that he is taking steps to thwart us, we must kill him. As much as I value his usefulness, *nothing* must jeopardize our plan to return California to the Mother Country."

14

At breakfast the next morning, Fargo saw McDade examining the Colt Navy revolver Fargo had given him back in Victoria. He closed one eye and squinted into the barrel.

"McDade," Fargo snapped, "if brains were horse shit, you'd have a clean corral."

"It's safe. I took the bullets out, Skye."

"So what? You never look down a barrel unless you've disassembled the weapon first. There's a rule you need to remember: 'Always look to your gun, but never let your gun look at you.' Have you had a lesson on shooting that weapon yet?"

The redheaded Irishman shook his head.

"It's high time you did. I have to ride out looking for water this morning. Cut out a horse and ride with me. We'll do a little plinking."

"All right. But why are you looking for water? You said we'd reach the Pecos River today."

"Rock this one to sleep, Mother," Booger said sarcastically. "Bitch, don't you know *nothing* about the West? You can't drink outta the Pecos Stream or you'll get the runny shits for days. 'At sumbitch is alkaline."

"It's all right for the livestock, though," Fargo added, "so let them tank up."

Miranda and Katrina were no longer allowed to eat with the Americans and were now taking their meals in their tent. But as Miranda carried her dishes to the wreck pan, she managed to pass close to Fargo.

"Have your binoculars ready at eight p.m.," she whispered to him. "Watch the fly of the tent."

She was gone a few moments later, trailing a teasing odor

of lilac perfume. But Booger had seen her whisper something to Fargo.

"May you rot in hell, Trailsman," he snarled. "Old Booger is horny as a Texas toad and once again you'll be combing pussy hairs outta them pretty teeth. I hope that little strumpet gives you the French pox."

"Look who's feeling a mite scratchy today."

"Ah, go piss up a rope."

After the Quintana party was under way, Fargo and McDade rode out bearing northwest from the trail.

"This morning, just after sunup," Fargo explained, "I saw flocks of birds headed this way. Birds go to water at first light, so maybe we'll get lucky."

The terrain thereabouts was mostly low sand hills covered with creosote and prickly pear. The transparency of the air in the Southwest made the Guadalupe Mountains, still a good hundred miles off, stand out so distinctly that they seemed within an easy hour's riding distance.

It was this extremely clear atmosphere that revealed dense black smoke rising from one of the mountain peaks.

"Look!" McDade pointed. "Something's burning in the mountains!"

"Moccasin telegraph," Fargo replied. "Watch it for a minute. Those are Indian smokes."

Within the next few minutes the smoke signals traveled from peak to peak in rapid succession.

"Can you read the signals, Skye?" McDade asked.

Fargo shook his head. "Never met a white man who could, not even a mountain man. Each tribe has its own signals and they guard them close. They signal when enemies or strangers enter their ranges. And sometimes a hunting party will signal, if they've been gone a long while and the rest have moved, so they know where to find them."

"Could they be signaling about us—the entire party approaching, I mean?"

"Could be. They follow troop movements close, and after that bloodbath back near San Antone, it's likely they consider this bunch troops."

"They're wise to do so," McDade said somberly. "Spanish troops on American soil, no less."

Fargo grunted. "It's all one to them. They consider this their land, and all white men are foreign invaders. Let's stow the chin-wag and give you that shooting lesson."

Fargo was surprised at how quickly McDade caught on to the basics of aiming and shooting a short gun. He had a steady hand and an unerring eye, and within ten minutes he was able to clip the tip off a cactus at fifty paces.

"You'll do to take along," Fargo praised. "But work on pointing and shooting faster—most times taking a long aim will get you plugged."

Ten minutes later they rounded the shoulder of a hill.

"You were right!" McDade exclaimed, pointing to a clutch of rocks with water frothing up among them. "An underground spring."

But Fargo was looking at something else—fresh tracks and fresh horse droppings surrounding the spring.

He swung down and studied the tracks first.

McDade joined him. "I see the horses are shod. How many riders?"

The tracks crossed one another in a confusing maze. Patiently Fargo worked out each set from the overlaps.

"At least eight, maybe ten riders," he finally said. "The prints are still pretty firm at the edges—made within the last day, I'd say."

He broke open some of the droppings with the toe of his boot and studied them. "They're graining their horses."

"Soldiers?"

"Could be a patrol. But it could also be El Lobo Flaco and his bunch. This is about the size of his gang, and outlaws stay on the move and rarely have time to graze their mounts."

McDade looked nervously around him. "I figured they gave up on us by now."

"I didn't," Fargo replied grimly. "The Skinny Wolf knows we'll be short on water, and somebody could be watching this spot. Let's let our horses drink and get back to camp."

Soon after they pointed their bridles southeast to intercept the rest, the hills gave way to an arid flat flanked by two low, rocky spines. Only a minute later the Ovaro pricked its ears forward.

"Trouble's on the spit," Fargo called over to McDade,

jerking the Henry from its saddle sheath. "Rate that gelding at a two-twenty clip!"

Even as Fargo fell silent, a plume of sand puffed up just a few feet in front of him, followed by the reverberating crack of a rifle. Riders came boiling out from behind the rocky spine to their left, rifles spitting orange spear tips of flame.

Both horsebackers ki-yied their mounts from a canter to a gallop, then a run. Soon the hard chase was on in earnest. At first the wide lead held in favor of Fargo and McDade. The Ovaro stretched out his long neck and lengthened his powerful stride, hindquarters sinking deep, muscles flexing with machine precision.

The Ovaro could easily have left the pursuers eating his dust. But the dish-faced ginger McDade had cut out from the saddle band possessed no such bottom. The gelding began to blow foam, then to falter, and Fargo knew McDade was a gone beaver if they kept it a horse race.

"Rein back a notch but keep going!" Fargo shouted to his companion. "I'll catch up to you!"

McDade, the freckles standing out in his tense, ashen face, nodded. Fargo wheeled the Ovaro and reined him to a standstill. He worked the Henry's lever and sprawled backward against his cantle. He swung his right leg up and hooked it around the saddle horn to anchor it. His rifle thus held steady when he laid the barrel across his thigh.

Rounds snapped past all around him, one grazing his saddle fender. But Fargo dropped a bead on one of the riders out front, took in a breath, and expelled it slowly as his finger squeezed through the slack.

The Henry bucked into his shoulder, and the Mexican he had notched onto threw his arms up toward the sky, the surprised stare of death etched into his face. Then he was jounced out of the saddle and sent tumbling head over heels across the barren ground.

"*That* kissed the mistress!" Fargo bragged to his stallion. After Fargo wiped a second man from the saddle, the Skinny Wolf and his cutthroats reversed their dust.

But as Fargo reined the Ovaro around to catch up with McDade, he cursed the luck. The Skinny Wolf might or might not have given up on heisting the viceroy's riches, but clearly he intended to finish the job he had botched a year ago in the Pecos country—the job of freeing Skye Fargo from his soul.

Salazar sent five of his best troops north with wooden casks to the water source Fargo had located. As the Quintana party continued westward, the day heated up under a merciless west Texas sun. The air felt hot as molten glass, and body sweat evaporated the moment it seeped from pores.

Booger, who reveled in the suffering of others, noticed how the parching heat was bothering Deke Lafferty. In one especially hot and dusty stretch, he bellowed out from the box of the lavish coach:

> *Thirty miles to water,*
> *Twenty miles to wood,*
> *Ten miles to hell,*
> *Deke's gone there for good!*

Fargo saw Miranda's fetching face appear in a coach window. "Mr. McTeague, must you always be shouting so?"

"Well, now, sugar britches, there's some little sneaks as likes to whisper, eh?"

Fargo tugged left rein until he was riding close beside Booger.

"Cut the cackle, you damn fool," he muttered. "Are you trying to get the girl in trouble with her father?"

"I? And what are *you* up to with her, Catfish? Temperance lectures? Gerlong there, mules! G'long! *Whoop!*"

Fargo felt a twinge of guilt because for once Booger was right. Whatever the saucy little beauty had planned for eight p.m. would certainly be risky—obviously she thrived on risk and the thrill of getting caught. But Fargo intended to be there with binoculars in hand. He had seen this young work of art naked, and that had been too long ago—the Siren's song was sapping his will to be cautious.

But neither had Fargo forgotten that the Skinny Wolf was in the area. Now and then he halted the party while he took to the highest point of land and studied the terrain carefully.

He spotted no signs of danger. But he made sure that Rivera never got behind him. The kill glint glowed in that man's fanatical eyes.

Bitch Creek McDade was driving the forage wagon. Fargo dropped back beside him.

"We'll be crossing the Pecos in about an hour," Fargo said.

"That's one thing I know about, Skye—fording rivers. We can raise the wagon beds between the uprights and hold them in that position by—"

Fargo laughed and raised a hand to silence him. "There's a reason, Bitch, why they call it the Pecos *Stream*. We won't have any trouble fording. What I'm worried about is an ambush. It's dangerous terrain right around the river. Keep your eyes peeled and be ready to use that Colt Navy."

"You know, back in Powder-horn? Jerome Helzer told me and Deke this trip would be like a trip to Santa's lap. So far we've been attacked by killer cows and Comanches, ambushed by El Lobo Flaco, damn near poisoned back in Victoria, *and* we're surrounded by dangerous Spaniards who will likely kill us before we collect our final wages. The Wheel of Fortune is starting downward for me, Skye—maybe all of us."

Fargo's brow runneled in puzzlement. "The what?"

"The Wheel of Fortune. It's an old Irish notion that goes back to the Middle Ages in Ireland. My ma believed it guides every person's life. My wheel has been spinning upward for some time now. But once it spins to the very top, the only direction left is down."

"All due respect to your mother," Fargo replied, "but that's hogwash. On the frontier 'luck' is just preparation meeting with opportunity. The readiness is all. So just be ready, and to hell with counting on luck."

Fargo gigged the Ovaro ahead for the approach to the gravel ford the army had laid down across the narrow bed of the Pecos. Ahead, on the long slope leading down to the river valley, was a wall of deep cutbanks—places where spring flood erosion had dug out dry land channels. They offered excellent hiding places for anyone interested in killing without being seen.

As did that clutch of mossy boulders up ahead on the left,

capping a low headland Fargo had to pass. *Caught between the Devil and the deep blue sea . . .*

Fargo paused at the head of the slope and studied the narrow, serpentine loops of the river. Then he shucked out his Colt, clicked the hammer back, and walked the Ovaro forward.

He passed the wall of cutbanks, then the mossy boulders, without incident. But as he rounded a turn in the trail, his jaw slacked open in astonishment.

A tollgate now stretched across the road. And standing in front of it, three towheaded men, obviously brothers. All three men held old muzzle-loading rifles across the crook of their left arms.

Fargo opted for discretion over valor and leathered his Colt.

"Howdy, boys," Fargo called to them.

The brothers lowered their weapons.

"Howdy yourself," replied the man who appeared to be the oldest brother. He spoke with a Deep South twang. "People cross for free, but animals cost four bits a head."

"That's mighty enterprising of you," Fargo said. "But this is a public road built by the U.S. Army. They laid down the gravel for the ford, too."

"So what?" one of the younger brothers demanded belligerently. "They don't bother to keep it in good repair. We do that."

"Well, I'm just the scout for a party coming up right behind me. I don't mind laying out four bits to keep the peace. But this group behind me—they got scores of animals. And they're not all as agreeable as I am. They'll insist that you fellows stand down."

"Not by a jugful, mister. They best pony up or we'll be down on them like all wrath."

By now Booger had pulled the coach up behind Fargo. He kicked the brake forward and heaved his considerable bulk down. All three brothers gaped in astonishment at sight of this man mountain.

"H'ar, now!" Booger roared out. "The hell's going on here, Fargo?"

"These gents are demanding toll. People cross free, they say, but each animal will cost four bits."

"So it's highway robbery, is it?" Booger demanded. "Well, *I'm* your daisy! Which one of you greasy little shit stains will beat four bucks outta Booger McTeague to cover them mules?"

None of them replied.

"Sing, minstrels!"

Nobody offered a tune.

"You got a fish bone caught in your throat, b'hoys? P'r'aps a paster on the nose will enlighten you."

Fargo bit back a grin. Hernando Quintana debouched from the coach, his face amiable. "Gentlemen, fifty cents for each of our animals is unreasonable. Would you be agreeable to a group fee of, say, five dollars in gold?"

The brothers suddenly became more charitable.

"Done," the oldest one agreed. He spotted the women inside the coach and lowered his voice so only Fargo and Booger could hear.

"Why not go the whole hog, boys?"

He pointed toward a low split-slab structure back in a circle of juniper trees. "We're runnin' a whorehouse, groggery, and gun shop, all on one stick. Good pussy, good antifogmatic, and hand-crimped ammo, none of this factory-pressed shit that misfires half the time."

Booger perked up. "Good pussy, you say? White women?"

"The only one we got is a toothless old Navajo. But, mister, she is *willing*. Only two bucks and you can go as many whacks as you like."

"Hmm . . ." Booger rubbed his chin, mulling the prospect. "No teeth, eh? I like a smooth bore."

Quintana had climbed back into the coach. Now he poked his head outside. "Senor McTeague, I do not know what the whispering is all about. But please put this coach in motion at once."

"You goddamn, highfalutin big bug," Booger muttered as he hopped up onto the box and snatched his whip from the socket.

He glowered at Fargo. "Yes, you grin, Catfish, you diabolical son of a bitch. Long as you get your ration, eh, slyboots? Old Booger will not forget how you rejoiced at his torment. Gerlong there, mules! *Whoop!*"

15

As usual Fargo and Booger spread their blankets that night near the rope corral with Bitch Creek McDade. Deke Lafferty had taken to sleeping on the chuck wagon in a futile attempt to protect the food and liquor from the two Indians, who nonetheless somehow managed to steal right from under his nose.

"Time you got, Bitch?" Fargo said.

McDade checked his pocket watch in the flickering torchlight. "Almost eight."

"Time for Fargo to top Miranda," Booger groused, "while the rest of us get the little end of the horn. It's bath night."

"I won't be topping anything," Fargo said, pulling his binoculars from a saddle pocket and rising to his feet. "Have you forgot about the guard watching the tent?"

"Spyglass?" Booger sat up. "After dark? Curioser and curioser . . . I seen Miranda whisper to you earlier. I'm stringing along with you, pretty teeth."

"Don't be hemming me," Fargo snapped as he buckled his gun belt on. "And quit banging your gums about how horny you are. I told you I'm not your damn pimp."

McDade waded in. "He's right, Booger. If the women were climbing all over you, would you worry about Fargo getting some of it?"

"Walk your chalk, you *reasonable* son of a bitch. I will not abide any man who resorts to logic."

Fargo left the two of them arguing and made his way to one of the supply wagons parked about twenty yards in front of the tent. He crouched down behind the tailgate. As usual, one of the Spanish soldiers, his Volcanic Arms repeating rifle at shoulder arms, paced in a wide, slow circle around the tent.

The torchlight was especially bright around the tent, and Fargo hardly needed binoculars to see that far. But he followed Miranda's instructions and fine-focused the binoculars on the closed fly of the tent.

As soon as the guard had finished passing in front of the tent, the flap was whipped aside and Fargo felt hot blood flood his tool in an insistent, pounding surge: Miranda, sleek and naked, stood boldly showing herself to him. The 7X binoculars seemed to bring her taut, pink-tipped breasts only inches away from his mouth.

A moment later Katrina, likewise a naked temptress, joined her.

Miranda beckoned him to join them.

Fargo, so hard he had to tuck at the knees to give his throbbing manhood more room, shook his head in disbelief. Was the girl *that* reckless?

When he hesitated, Miranda upped the erotic ante. She tugged the fly closed just long enough to let the sentry pass on his next round. It opened again and this time she sat in a canvas camp chair, thighs spread wide. She used both slim white hands to spread her love nest open wide, giving Fargo a magnificent and magnified view of her coral grotto.

"God*damn*," Fargo muttered, his resolve weakening as he studied the pink, mysterious petals and folds of her most intimate femininity. Her pearl nubbin was swollen in anticipation.

She raised one hand to beckon again, and the last vestige of Fargo's resistance crumbled like a sand castle in angry surf.

He waited until the guard's next pass and then bolted forward like a bronc exploding out of the chute. He just barely beat the guard's notice, tumbling headlong into the tent as Miranda closed the fly again.

"I knew you'd come!" Miranda whispered excitedly, tugging his shirt off even before Fargo was on his feet. "Come feel this, Katrina!"

Both naked beauties ran their hands over his muscle-corded shoulders and an upper body hard as sacked salt.

Katrina opened his trousers and the two women took turns stroking his shaft.

"We can both put our hands around it at the same time!" Miranda marveled.

Fargo groaned appreciatively as their ministrations sent hot tickling currents of pleasure through him. Each of his hands played with a set of gorgeous tits.

"I thought you only like to exhibit and watch," he teased Miranda.

"Watching is exactly what I'm going to do," she assured him in her eager, take-charge manner that excited Fargo. "You're going to lick my valentine while Katrina sucks you off, and I'm going to watch all of it right there!"

She pointed to a dressing mirror propped against a clothing trunk. A camp stool sat in front of it.

"Or do you, like most men," she said, "refuse to pleasure a woman with your mouth?"

"I give as good as I get," Fargo assured her.

So excited she was wiggling like a puppy, Miranda tugged Fargo and Katrina into place.

She sat on the stool. "You get on your knees in front of me, Skye. Katrina will lie sideways on that quilt between the two of us. Oh, hurry, both of you! I've been dreaming about this for weeks."

She opened those sleek, shapely thighs. The moment Fargo had dropped his gun belt and was kneeling before her, she laced her fingers at the back of his head and pulled his face into her nest. Fargo felt the lush, warm heat of her desire as he wrapped his tongue around her pleasure button.

Katrina, propped up on one elbow between their legs, took his swollen purple glans into her mouth, working it magnificently by tightening her lips and swirling her tongue on it.

Fargo flicked his tongue rapidly like a snake sampling the air, feeling the pearl button swell tighter and tighter. Miranda was in ecstasy as she watched all this in the mirror, wiggling her taut butt and gasping as climaxes almost immediately began to wash over her in tidal waves of pleasure.

Katrina whimpered in excitement as she felt Fargo expanding to an iron hardness in her mouth.

"That's it, Katrina!" Miranda egged her one, eyes fixated

on the erotic tableau in the mirror. "Faster! Move your head faster! Suck him harder! Swing his sac out so I can see it better-r-r—*Oh!*"

The mother of all climaxes ripped through her in intense spasms as Fargo felt his own floodgates bursting open. He jettisoned and collapsed in Miranda's lap, her silken bush caressing his face as they panted.

When his strength returned, Fargo rose and buckled on his gun belt, then donned his shirt.

"Ladies, thank you for a fine visit. But, Katrina, you're the duenna here and I want you to talk this young lady out of any more shenanigans like tonight. It's too dangerous."

"Oh, the *danger* makes it so much better, Skye," Miranda insisted.

Fargo grinned as he parted the tent flaps slightly to glance outside. "You hot little firecracker, you'll get us all killed."

Fargo waited until the sentry glided past and then bolted back toward the supply wagon. But in his hurry he didn't see the small rock his left foot landed on, sending him sprawling. He regained his feet and dived for the wagon. A second later the challenge sounded behind him:

"*Alta! Quien va?*"

Fargo had no idea if the sentry had seen him or just heard him fall. But if he tried to hoof it back to the rope corral, he'd be spotted in all this light. Nor could he remain here, silent, and let the sentry catch him. He decided to run a bluff.

"It's Fargo. I'm just taking a leak."

"But I saw you just now leap behind the wagon. And you came from the direction of the tent."

"You are mighty mistaken. How could I get to or from the tent without you spotting me?"

"I did spot you."

The sentry stood still for perhaps twenty seconds, unsure what to do and saying nothing more. Then he resumed his pacing.

But Fargo cursed his bad luck. These Spanish soldiers were as loyal as the Praetorian Guard, and this one would surely report this to Quintana and Salazar. Fargo knew the exaggerated pride and "honor" of these Spaniards. One way or another, this serious affront to their manliness—especially Salazar's—would have to be answered.

"Yessir," Fargo muttered to himself as he headed back to his bedroll, "there's no such thing as easy money."

Five days after Fargo's pleasant tryst in the tent, the Quintana party rolled through El Paso del Norte and into the vast New Mexico Territory.

Fargo knew it as the land of bloodred suns and pale ghost moons, of winds that shrieked like souls in pain and a place where death was as swift as an eyeblink—the land of Kit Carson and Coronado and Montezuma, a beautiful, awful land of red and purple mesas and whitewater falls and bone-dry *jornadas* that dried a man to jerky. The land from out whose terrible depths men were seasoned or driven mad.

Fargo had searched out the farther reaches of the American West, knew every state and territory and mountain range and river. But New Mexico cast a spell over him like no other place he knew, for no other place was quite like it.

"Boys," he announced to his companions during breakfast, "we'll make Las Cruces before nightfall barring any trouble. That's three days to resupply, recruit the animals, and live high on the hog at the Montezuma House."

"Clean sheets," McDade said.

"Good food and liquor," Deke said.

"Smoke-eyed whores flirting from behind them fancy fans," Booger chipped in. "Oh, Lulu girl!"

Fargo nodded. "Yeah, all that and the old viceroy pays the freight for everything 'cept maybe the sporting gals. But it won't be all beer and skittles—I can almost guarandamntee the Skinny Wolf and his greasy-sack outfit will be waiting there, and he'll likely make his play at the hotel."

"Pull up your skirts, Nancy," Booger scoffed. "Hell, he won't be expectin' us to flop at diggings that fancy. Why, the rooms alone is five dollars a night!"

"Yeah, but you're forgetting—at the time old man Quintana told us about staying there, Rivera could still have been in cahoots with the Skinny Wolf. Besides, I think Quintana likely told the unholy trinity about it long before he told us."

"And don't forget, Booger," McDade tossed in, "me and Fargo were attacked by El Lobo less than a week ago."

Booger relented with a nod. "Aye, he's plenty dangersome. But it's mainly Fargo he's thirsting to kill, so why do us three give a hoot? With Fargo feeding worms, there'll be more quim for us."

"Look on the bright side," Fargo agreed sarcastically.

"Fargo, you got more on your plate'n just that Mex outlaw," Deke said, nodding across the camp toward Captain Diego Salazar and his companions. "Used to was, it was only Rivera who kept givin' you the hoodoo eye. But *look* at that son of a buck Salazar—God dawg! He's fixin' to catawumptiously chaw you up."

Booger grinned maliciously. "That's on account Fargo trimmed his woman. Got caught, too. I heard the guard challenge the randy bastard when he slipped outta the tent."

"What's the difference?" McDade said. "They mean to kill all of us. The prize for them is California, not Skye Fargo. We'd better all hope *nobody* kills him because he's our only chance—and California's, too."

The Quintana party rolled into the outskirts of the dusty, sleepy adobe settlement of Las Cruces about two hours before sundown. Fargo made arrangements to park the conveyances behind the livery where the horses and mules were boarded. Quintana paid two stable boys generously to keep an eye on the coach night and day.

Yellow-brown desert surrounded the town, dotted with low mesas, with purple-tinged mountains to the northwest. The town had been long established because of its key location on the long trade route known as the King's Highway, linking Santa Fe and points east to Chihuahua, Durango, and Aguascalientes in deep Mexico.

Quintana had paid an exorbitant price to reserve two entire floors of the Montezuma House for three days, telegraphing from El Paso to announce their imminent arrival. Fargo was astounded by such luxurious opulence this far west: marble-top tables, four-poster beds, velvet draperies, beveled-glass mirrors, and English china in the dining room.

The four men turned all their dirty clothing in at the hotel laundry, then stood guard in pairs when they visited the luxurious bathhouse, soaking off the layers of trail dust. They killed the half hour until dinner by strolling the wide streets of Las Cruces.

McDade goggled at the huge, unwieldy, high-sided carts pitching and heaving clumsily through the streets.

"Those are Mexican carts called wheeled tarantulas," Fargo said, "because of those uneven wooden wheels. But don't get caught up in the sights too much. I see plenty of Mexican men glomming us, and some of 'em could be the Skinny Wolf's lunatic hyenas waiting for the first chance to burn us down."

The center of the town was a big plaza used for a *mercado* or street market. Deke pointed to a group of six or seven Mexican girls sitting at one edge of the plaza. Huge *ristras*, strings of dried red peppers, were piled all around them. They were all using mortars and pestles to crush the pods into fine powder. Gunnysacks behind them were packed tight with the ground pepper.

"I'm gonna buy some of that before we leave town," Deke said. "No cook should be without it. It's the best chili powder in the world, and it's growed only in New Mexico. Mighty potent stuff."

The wind suddenly gusted just as Fargo was passing one of the girls. A small red puff of ground powder blew up from her mortar and pestle.

Intense heat suddenly invaded Fargo's eyes, and immediately he suffered from tearing eyes and blurred vision.

Deke snorted. "Keep upwind from that shit. Them 'ere chili peps is murder on a feller's eyes."

"Damn," Fargo said, still trying to clear his vision. "It priddy near blinded me, and it was only a little puff."

"That stuff isn't food—it's a weapon," McDade joked. "Good thing the Skinny Wolf didn't jump you while you were blinded."

Fargo started to reply. Abruptly he fell silent and looked thoughtful. A moment later, however, he pushed the foolish notion from his mind.

They were strolling back along the opposite side of the plaza when Fargo spotted a white-haired old woman selling a variety of odd-shaped gourds. He selected two that were large and nearly round.

"The hell you want with such truck?" Booger demanded.

"Humor me," Fargo said. "I'm eccentric. Boys, let's head back to the hotel and get outside some fancy grub. But first I want to stop by the livery where we left the horses and mules."

"What for?" Deke asked.

"We're going to clip some hair from the mules' tails."

"Catfish," Booger said, "have you been visiting the peyote soldiers?"

"Nope," Fargo replied. "I'm just getting ready for what will come."

16

It was three a.m., and Juan Lopez, the night clerk at the Montezuma House, was dozing in a chair behind the broad mahogany counter in the lobby. Suddenly something hard and sharp pressed into his windpipe and he woke with a start.

The first thing the confused clerk saw was a skinny man with a face stretched tight against his skull and a lipless grin like a turtle's. The man beside him had a face pitted with old smallpox scars. Someone standing behind Lopez held a huge knife tight against his neck.

"Madre de Dios," the clerk whispered hoarsely. Piss suddenly squirted down his leg when he realized the grinning man was El Lobo Flaco, the notorious Skinny Wolf.

"Por favor," the clerk begged, *"no me mata. Tengo una marida y tres hijos."*

"I am not here to kill you," the Skinny Wolf said. "And you will return safely to your wife and children if you do what you are told. *Entiendes?"*

Lopez swallowed the huge lump in his throat and nodded. "I understand."

"Bueno. Skye Fargo is staying in this hotel. Give me the key to his room."

When Lopez, too paralyzed with fear to move, hesitated, the Skinny Wolf nodded once to the man with the knife. The blade pressed harder.

"It is room 314," the clerk hastened to say, pointing to the board loaded with keys on the wall beside him.

The Skinny Wolf snatched the key down. "Does he have his own room?"

Lopez shook his head. "No. Senor Quintana's people are

133

assigned two to a room. There is a giant gringo sharing Fargo's room."

El Lobo looked at Ramon Velasquez and both men grinned.

"The fat man," El Lobo said. "Better and better. Pedro told me he is the blowhard who threatened to kill him at the Alibi Saloon in Victoria."

"Check the book, *jefe*," Velasquez suggested. "Perhaps this one gave us the wrong key."

El Lobo grinned. "Look . . . this soft-handed coward has pissed himself. He gave us the right key. *Matalo, Paco.*"

With one deep, hard slice the blade expert opened the clerk's throat and then threw him onto the floor, leaving him to choke to death on his own blood.

"Now we end it for good with Fargo," the Skinny Wolf told his men, drawing the .41-caliber magazine pistol from the canvas holster under his left armpit. "He has made his vow to kill me, and so long as he is above the horizon we will never be safe."

The three men moved swiftly to the stairs at the back of the lobby and ascended to the third floor. Lamps in brass wall sconces softly lighted the hallway.

They stopped at the door of room 314. For a long time the Skinny Wolf stood with his ear pressed to the door, listening.

Finally he looked at his companions and nodded.

Working with infinite care and patience, the Skinny Wolf stood to one side and inserted the key, slowly turning it. When it finally clicked softly, he waited a full two minutes.

"Wait here," he whispered to Paco.

Slowly, one cautious inch at a time, he eased the door open. Enough light seeped into the room to illuminate two beds. He could see the two sleeping men clearly outlined under crisp white sheets, the mound on the right huge.

Their heads lay against the pillows. Paco already had his instructions. In just moments one of those heads would be severed, later to be preserved in brine and displayed all over the Southwest and Mexico. No man would be more famous—and feared—than the one who could prove he killed the famous Trailsman.

The Skinny Wolf felt elation rising within him like a tight bubble. It would be easier than plucking two birds' nests off the ground.

He caught Velasquez's eyes and nodded toward the sleeping giant. Velasquez nodded back.

The two men cat-footed a few paces into the room.

Why, a voice from the depths of El Lobo's mind whispered, *can you not hear either of them snoring?* But in his heady elation the voice did not quite rise to the level of suspicion.

"Ahora, Ramon!"

They opened fire simultaneously, their pistols obscenely loud and shocking in the stillness and peace of the sleeping hotel. Taking no chances, both men emptied their guns into the men in the beds.

"De prisa, Paco!" the Skinny Wolf ordered. "Hurry! Take his head! This hotel is filled with armed soldiers."

The moment Paco spurted into the room, the double doors of a large closet banged open.

"I'm not the type to lose my head, Lobo," Fargo greeted the startled Mexican before his Colt barked in his fist.

The top of the Skinny Wolf's skull lifted off as neatly as the lid of a tobacco jar, releasing a pebbly spray of blood and brains. The Mexican outlaw's knees buckled like an empty sack and the body flopped into a twitching heap.

Booger didn't need to bother with a head shot. The Colt Dragoon's huge, conical ball ripped through Ramon Velasquez's chest and knocked him backward with the force of an iron fist, dead before he hit the floor.

Paco turned to bolt for the door. Fargo shot him in the left side. When the force of the slug spun him around, Fargo drilled him through the heart.

"I hate to shoot a man in the back," he explained to Booger as he turned up a lamp on the dresser.

The extra illumination revealed that the "heads" on the pillows were the two gourds Fargo had purchased earlier, mule-tail hair glued to the top of them. Quilts and blankets had been stuffed under the sheets in the rough outline of human bodies.

Fargo heard a commotion of rapid footsteps and confused

voices in the hallway. The first two faces that peered cautiously into the smoke-hazed room were Deke Lafferty and Bitch Creek McDade, who were staying in the adjacent room. The heavy, acrid stench of spent powder made them wrinkle their noses.

McDade stared at the three men lying on the floor, their blood soaking the Persian rugs. "Are they . . . ?"

"Dead as they come," Fargo assured him.

"The Skinny Wolf?" Deke asked, still buttoning his suspender loops to his trousers.

Fargo nodded. "And that plug-ugly cuss with the pockmarks is Ramon Velasquez, his *segundo*. Can't tell you who the third one is, but it was his job to lop off my head for a souvenir."

"The outlaws get the headlines," McDade said, "and the working man gets the outlaws. Good work, gents."

"Yeah, but I guess we'll hafta drag them out," Deke said reluctantly. "And from the third floor."

"Nix on that, Catfish," Booger said. "Old Booger has not been asleep all night and needs his rest. They have trash collection in this fine city, and there's a big, empty lot next door."

He lumbered over to the window casement and swung the panes open. As effortlessly as if he were picking up sacks of rags, he tossed all three corpses outside.

By now a crowd had gathered outside the door. Diego Salazar, wearing only his gold-braided trousers, pushed his way into the room.

"What is going on here?" he demanded as if he had a right to know.

Fargo wagged his Colt at him. "I expect you'll read about it tomorrow in the newspaper. Now clear out, all of you, so me and this ugly knight of the ribbons can grab some sleep."

Salazar, who had been seething with brooding hatred since the night Fargo was spotted near the tent, tightened his lips grimly. "You will regret pointing that weapon at me."

"Oh, we'll be hugging," Fargo agreed. He thumbed back the hammer. "Now clear out before I *buck* you out."

Fargo's victory over the Skinny Wolf was not without consequences.

The discovery of the murdered hotel clerk and the damage caused to Fargo's room by the flurry of bullets did not endear the Quintana party to the manager of the highly respectable Montezuma House.

The final straw came when it was learned that the lurid tale of frontier violence, wildly "colored up" by a local ink slinger, had been released to the Associated Press, established a decade earlier for the sharing of telegraphic dispatches. Skye Fargo's shooting scrapes were popular newspaper fare back in the land of steady habits, and now the staid Montezuma House was depicted as yet another Wild West hellhole.

"Quintana is fit to be tied," Bitch Creek McDade reported on their second night in Las Cruces. "He was ordered to pull up stakes and move everyone out by tomorrow morning."

"Pah! Me'n Skye should just let ourselves be killed in our beds?" Booger protested. "And why not make us eat shit and go naked, too?"

He sighed tragically. "By the Lord Harry! One less night of whoring for old Booger."

"In a town with a right smart chance of pretty girls," Deke added. "These twirling *chiquitas* in Las Cruces could make a dead man come."

Fargo paid scant attention to this piffle. The four men shared a table in the hotel saloon, a fancy watering hole with a long, S-shaped bar and two bartenders in octagonal ties and gaitered sleeves. But it was the table next to them that held his attention.

Salazar, Aragon, and Rivera had just entered, deliberately ignoring the many other empty tables to sit close by. Their grim, humorless faces told him they were spoiling for a fight.

Booger suddenly grabbed Fargo's beer. He took a sweeping-deep slug, then wiped the white foam off his upper lip with the back of his hand.

"Faugh! It's naught but warm piss with bubbles. Why'n't you drink whiskey like a man?"

Fargo glanced at the half-empty bottle of rye in front of Booger. "You'd better rein in, old son. It's not even dark yet, and you'll soon be walking on your knees."

"Say—look at Rivera," McDade cut in, keeping his voice low.

The Spanish sergeant made a big show of slipping a bracelet of curved horseshoe nails over his knuckles—"drinking jewelry" as they were called by American soldiers. He spoke in a loud voice intended for the four men at the next table, fixing his small, piglike eyes on Fargo as he spoke.

"There are two places, Capitan Salazar, where a hard, well-aimed punch with these almost always kills: at the hollow between a man's eyes and at the little bone ridge in front of each ear just below the temples."

"Let it go, Booger," Fargo muttered urgently when the big man started to scrape his chair back. "They're deliberately goading us. If we kill them now, those soldiers will execute us before we can break up Quintana's plot."

"Crikes! How'm I spozed to sit still for that shit?"

"Don't rise to his bait," Deke scoffed. "That beat-down Fargo give him a while back is still ranklin' in his craw. He's alla time a-puffin' and a-blowin'."

"Aye, but he best sing small or I'll row him up Salt River."

When Rivera's little show failed to rile the Americans sufficiently, Lieutenant Juan Aragon waded in.

"This vast land called New Mexico—the *norteamericanos* declared it a territory in 1850. But centuries before, it was a northern province of New Spain. Santa Fe hosted kings and queens before the dirt-grubbing 'pilgrims' cleared the first trees beside the Atlantic Ocean. Now these unwashed pigs turn our beautiful women into whores and spit their filthy tobacco on ancient floors of marble."

"Cut the waterworks," Booger scoffed despite Fargo's warning, for Captain Cup had him in his grip. "New Spain my hairy white ass! The Mexers chased you Dagos out first. It was them pepper-guts we stole New Mexico from, not you prissy Espanish fops. All you silly sons a' bitches done was chase around lookin' for cities of gold. You stupid bastards couldn't locate your own assholes with two hands and a lantern."

"Sew up your damn lips," Fargo muttered. "We *don't* want the fandango now."

But by now a drunken Booger was wound up to a faire-thee-well, and his penchant for bad puns got the best of him.

"I seen all three of you catamites sneering at the whores last night. S'matter—is poking soiled doves *Benicia dignity*?"

A cold hand gripped Fargo's heart as all three Spaniards reacted as if they'd been slapped hard. As one man they rose and hurried upstairs.

McDade spoke first. "Booger McTeague, you drunken Irish sot. Now they know that *we* know."

"Are you soft twixt your head handles?" Deke demanded. "We're in for a heap o' misery now."

Booger, instantly sobered by the magnitude of what he had just done, looked thoroughly chastened—a rare state for him. "Aye, old Booger just screwed the pooch."

"Never mind," Fargo snapped. "There'll be time to shoot you later. Boys, it's come down to the nut-cuttin' now. I don't think they'll try to kill us tonight. They'll wait until we're all on the trail again and they can turn all their guns on us. So the four of us are going to light a shuck out of Las Cruces tonight. Deke?"

"Yo!"

"The *mercado* should still be open. I want you to ske-daddle over there and buy a full gunnysack of that chili powder that damn near blinded me."

"But—"

"Stick your damn 'butts' back in your pocket. All three of you, listen up. We're in a mighty dirty corner now. I'm making the medicine and you're taking it—I want no questions. Just do what you're told. Booger. . . ."

"Yes, Skye," the miscreant said meekly.

"You know where Cherokee Bob and All Behind Him are holed up. Ride out and tell them to head for Diablo Canyon—Bob knows where it is. Tell them we're up against it bad and they have to go *now* and wait for us there."

Fargo turned to McDade. "Bitch, there's a gun and ammo shop over on Silver Street. The owner is a big Swede named Olney. The place will be closed now, but Olney lives in a room at the rear of the shop. Knock on the back door and tell him Fargo sent you—he'll open back up. I'll make out a list of the ammo we need."

The stakes, Fargo realized, could not be higher. One stupid, drunken pun had just changed everything—perhaps even crippled a young nation. One careless word, the *wrong* word, and now the danger clock was set ticking.

Death had still been a distant prospect before Booger's drunken slip. Now it was as real as a man beside them, one breathing down their necks and liable to strike at any moment.

And if Death succeeded this time, far more was at stake than the lives of four men.

17

The clock in the city plaza chimed two a.m.

"We can't wait any longer," Fargo told Booger. "I told Deke and McDade to sneak out by midnight and wait for us near the livery. We want to get a good lead on Quintana's bunch. We've got about seventy miles of hard riding across one of the worst *jornadas* in the territory. We'll have to spell our mounts often, and they won't hold up in that desert sun if we rate them faster than a trot."

Fargo turned the lamp down and crossed to the window casement. He eased it open just enough to glance down.

"He's still there. Quintana is determined to keep the net around us."

Fargo turned the wick up again. Booger sat on the edge of his bed and built himself a smoke.

"The hell's the deal with this Diablo Canyon?"

"It's a red-rock canyon due west of Las Cruces. I learned about it during a scout for the Army Topographical Corps. Navajos use it for a burial ground."

"Katy Christ! You know what happens to hair faces when the featherheads catch 'em in their sacred ground. That's heap bad medicine."

"Yeah," Fargo acknowledged, "but it's a chance we're going to take. Diablo Canyon is perfect for what I got in mind."

Fargo crossed to the door and slowly eased it open a crack.

"They've still got a guard by the stairs, too," he told Booger.

"Happens we do manage to sneak out, Skye, you know we *could* just liberate their horses."

"What good would it do? The viceroy is rich enough to buy every horse in the area. Remember, we're not trying to escape—we *have* to lock horns with them if we mean to put the kibosh on their plot."

Booger saw the truth of this and nodded. "Yes, for we have not one jot of proof we can take to the law or the army. We scatter their horses and we're just putting off a nasty job."

Booger licked the paper and quirled the ends of his cigarette. "Fargo, this child swears by all things holy—I'm powerful sorry for saying 'Benicia' in front of the garlics."

"Tell you the truth," Fargo replied, "I'm almost glad you did. I've been waffling about how to play this deal. Now you've forced their hand *and* ours. But let's stow the chin music and make our move."

Earlier, Bitch Creek McDade had delivered a pasteboard box filled with the cartons of ammo he had purchased. Fargo picked it up from the dresser and hefted it.

"We can't risk taking on that hallway guard," he said. "It would cause a commotion. And we can't shoot at the one below our window, either."

Booger caught on. "So we conk him on the *cabeza* with that box."

Fargo nodded. "It's plenty heavy. First let's rustle up a rope and get it ready."

Slicing their linen sheets into long strips, they knotted them together and tied one end to the steam radiator under their window. Fargo slowly eased the casement open and Booger handed him the box. The Spanish guard stood just to one side of the window and about ten feet out from the building.

"It's a tricky angle," Fargo muttered. "I got one chance to do it right or our cake is dough."

Fargo would have to push the box out as he dropped it, skewing it slightly left at the same time. He worked all the vectors out in his mind.

"Let 'er rip," Booger whispered.

Fargo released the ammo-weighted box. There was a hard *whumph* from below, a surprised grunt, and a second later the sentry lay heaped in the grass.

"I'll go down first," Fargo said, throwing the rope out and

142

tossing a leg over the sill. "For Christ sakes wait until I'm clear before you start down. If that rope breaks and you land on me, I'll be turned into a damned accordion."

When both men were safely on the ground, Booger gathered up the scattered boxes of ammo while Fargo quickly checked the guard.

"Broke his neck," Fargo said. "He's dead."

"Serves the bastard right. They mean to kill us."

"From here on out, no pity and no mercy," Fargo agreed. "These ain't just crooks—these jackleg soldiers are foreign invaders attacking a sovereign nation. I wish somebody else could skin this grizzly, but it's come down to us. C'mon."

"What if there was guards on Deke and Bitch?" Booger fretted as the two men headed for the livery on the outskirts of Las Cruces.

"I hate to say it," Fargo replied, "but that's not our lookout. I like both of them, but every man will have to pull his own freight from here on out. These Spaniards appear to have poor trail-craft, but even a blind hog could follow the trail we're about to leave—and they *will* follow it. We got one helluva fight brewing, Booger, against a passel of well-disciplined marksmen who know how to hold and squeeze."

"I know," Booger said joyfully. "Ain't it the berries?"

Fargo grinned in the dark. "It's a privilege to be here," he agreed.

Fargo gazed out across the desolate, shimmering vista. A distant spine of barren mountains seemed to melt and re-form in the blistering heat.

"Good God Almighty," McDade said. "I've read about deserts, but this is the first I've ever seen. Only nine o'clock in the morning and it's hotter than the hinges of hell."

"It'll get hotter," Fargo assured him.

This was a typical southern New Mexico *jornada*, a hot, barren expanse of alkali dirt. Nothing about this dead, desiccated terrain spoke of hope. In the distance Fargo occasionally saw a tall, narrow, pointy cactus known as Spanish bayonet; closer to hand was cracked and parched earth with scattered tufts of wiry *palomilla* grass, so worthless the horses scorned it.

Booger spat—or tried to. All his parched lips could produce was a pathetic, sputtering noise. His saddle ox, however, was enduring the heat better than the horses were. Nor was its slower speed a problem—the horses, by now, could barely hold a trot. Every hour the men were forced to spell them by dismounting and walking them for ten minutes.

"Christmas crackers! I'm spitting cotton," Booger complained. "Why'n't we share out a canteen?"

"Nix on that," Fargo said. "There's a spring at the bottom of Diablo Canyon. Until then we'll need every drop for the horses."

Fargo usually carried a goatskin water bag tied to his saddle horn, but when they tried to fill it at the livery, he had discovered a slit in the bottom—no doubt the handiwork of the Spaniards. The men had been forced to make do with filling their canteens.

Deke, the oldest of the four, was suffering the most. "How much farther?" he asked Fargo in a cracked voice.

"I figure we're about halfway," the Trailsman replied. "We're not exactly making jig time. And you might's well face it: the second half will be the worst, so buck up. That's why I wanted us to build a lead—we'll need to rest up."

Fargo pulled some pebbles out of a saddle pocket and gave each man a few of them. "Suck on these, boys. It'll help your mouth produce some moisture."

"I wonder if those two crazy Indians went on ahead like Booger told them," McDade said. "I'd wager they just cleared out and washed their hands of us. Why should they give a hoot about a white man's battle?"

"No, they followed orders," Fargo said. "You can see their tracks. Matter fact, they shoulda reached the canyon hours ago. They were riding at night."

"They don't give a damn whose battle it is," Booger said. "It's just, they're death on Deke's fine cooking."

"I'm just mighty glad to hear they'll be waiting," Deke said. "Them two red grifters are dangerous killers."

"Crick . . . crack," Booger said, and despite their suffering and the looming prospect of a hard death, all four men laughed.

Captain Diego Salazar looked slender in the saddle, but capable and bold, his neat mustaches now tipped with white dust that seemed to age him a few years.

Despite the furnace heat and unrelenting sun, he refused to remove his expensive frogged tunic of red velveteen. It, like his mustaches, was white with alkali dust. It was also unbuttoned and limp from dried sweat.

He rode his coal black Arabian, a desert horse by lineage, flanked on either side by Lieutenant Juan Aragon and Sergeant Miguel Rivera. The rest of his men followed in a tight double file.

"We are gaining on them," he told Aragon and Rivera. "Their dust is easier to see now. They have little water and their mounts must be near foundering."

"The long weeks of forbearance are over," Rivera said, a fervent glint to his eyes. "His Excellency has finally given us the order to kill Fargo. I have thirsted to do so since first laying eyes on this arrogant, godless pagan whom his nation's newspapers call the savage angel."

"Sergeant Rivera, you must *still* practice forbearance," Salazar said sternly. "Yes, you have just cause to kill him. But for me it is also an affair of personal honor. You know that he beguiled and seduced Miranda. Kill as many others as you will, but leave him for me. He has already promised me a duel, and the point of my sword is the period that will end his life."

"The Road of By and By," Aragon said, quoting an old Spanish proverb, "leads to the House of Never. Swift action first gave us this New World empire, and swift action is how we will return *Californio* to Spain. And eventually, perhaps, New Mexico with it."

"And swift action," Salazar added, "is how we will kill Fargo and the dogs who lick his hand. He is only a man, but a man surrounded by a legend. When I kill him, I will also kill the legend."

18

The glare from the sun on the hardpan and white alkali was unrelenting. Sweat eased out from Fargo's hairline and immediately evaporated. But the dust cloud boiling up behind them was rapidly growing closer.

"It ain't just that they got water and we ain't," Deke complained. "They *musta* got started before sunup to be this close."

Fargo had trouble, at first, moving his tongue to speak. He had to cope with the chalky grit coating the inside of his mouth, as well as dry lips cracked so deep they showed blood.

"Likely they found the dead sentry when a man was sent to relieve him," he replied.

"Are we gonna make it to that canyon before they catch us?" McDade asked, his face a freckled mask of worry.

"We will," Fargo said, his tone more confident than he felt. "It's only about three miles now."

He had grave doubts about their mounts. Booger's saddle ox was plugging patiently along, but the horses were sulky with exhaustion, even Fargo's Ovaro. The men had watered them from their hats for the last time ten miles back, and now the horses were at the scrag-end of their endurance. It was McDade, an excellent wrangler, who kept them moving, coaxing the trail-worn animals in the voice of a patient old friend.

"Fargo," Booger said, "you're the one's always saying how you druther be attacked out in the open where you can pick your enemies off before they get in close. Why'n't we just dig sand wallows and commence to busting caps when they're within range?"

"For one thing," Fargo replied, "that leaves us two men short—Cherokee Bob and All Behind Him. For another, these soldiers are on Quintana's payroll because they're dead shots. Even if we wrestle our mounts down, they make for big targets. Those Spaniards can hang back, kill the horses, and then throw a fiesta because that'll mean all of us are gone coons, too. How long you figure we'll survive out here afoot—and with no water?"

"'Bout as long as a snowball would last in hell," Booger admitted.

"We'll get to that canyon first," Fargo assured him. "And if we use it right, we'll turn the viceroy's big plans into brain vapors. Okay, boys, light down and spell your mounts."

The men, faces sagging with weariness, slid down and walked the animals for the next ten minutes. Fargo glanced from man to man: their eyes had that dull, bovine gaze caused by staring for long hours at open country without any reference points.

The sun had reached its zenith, the heat so fierce that "cook-offs"—bullets heat-detonated by the scorching metal of weapons—had become a risk. Fargo recalled a time, crossing the vicious Salt Desert of Utah, when a round had cooked off in the Henry's sun-heated tube magazine—he had damn near broken his neck when the spooked Ovaro chinned the moon and bucked him off.

"Unload your weapons," he called out, "and pocket the rounds. Our guns are blazing hot."

He swung out the cylinder of his Colt and emptied it before also emptying his spare cylinder and the Henry's magazine.

"What if them garlics catch up to us and we got nothing but our dicks in our hands?" Booger carped.

"When *ain't* your dick in your hand?" Deke quipped.

"Whenever Pretty Teeth here ain't around to hog all the quim."

Fargo's cracked lips eased into a grin. "Ain't my fault women got good taste in men. Anyhow, don't fret, Booger. We'll make it safe to that canyon and dip our weapons quick in the spring to cool them before we reload."

Still walking the Ovaro, he pulled out his binoculars to

147

study their back trail. The Spaniards were close enough now that he could recognize Salazar, Aragon, and Rivera, their faces as grim as Inquisitors under their tall shako hats.

Close and gaining. Fargo felt a prickle of alarm move up his spine in a tickling squiggle. Booger's ox, Ambrose, was holding up, but Deke and McDade's mounts were about blown in.

"Mount up!" he called. "As soon as you butt your saddles, Deke and Bitch, lean forward and bite your horse's ears—and bite 'em hard!"

Neither man questioned the order. The moment Fargo chomped into the Ovaro's tender ear, the enraged stallion surged forward, as did the other two horses. The burst of speed wasn't sustained long, but suddenly the lip of a vast, steep, redrock canyon hove into view up ahead on their right.

"By God, we made 'er!" Deke exclaimed. "*Hoo*-rah, boys!"

"Skye *said* we'd beat those devils," Deke said in a welter of elation.

"It's too early to tack up bunting," Fargo snapped. "We've got to hustle now. There's only one way in, and it's narrow, so follow me in single file. Booger, you're the rearguard. If anybody rides in behind us, shoot him to wolf bait."

A rocky, steeply descending Indian trace led down to the floor of the canyon. At some ancient time a river had cut the steep cliffs that formed its striated walls. Trap rock shelves had been carved out by wind in the centuries since, making the walls nearly impossible to scale, especially from above.

"This is the only way in," Fargo repeated as they descended. "If they mean to put paid to us, they'll have to ride this trail down. If it hasn't dried up, the spring is under that big trap rock shelf at the rear of the canyon."

"Say, Catfish," Booger called out from the rear, "if there's only one way in, there's only one way *out*. What if them sons of Coronado decide to just starve us out?"

"Then we'll be shit out of luck," Fargo admitted cheerfully. "But with water and horses to slaughter and eat, we could hold out for a month or so. Does that prideful hothead Salazar strike you as the type who's willing to wait?"

"Naw. He's the type to stick the reins in his teeth and come in a-smokin'."

"God *dawg*!" Deke exclaimed a few minutes later when they emerged onto the floor of the canyon. His horse shied back at the spooky sight.

"Stick your eyes back in your head," Fargo said. "I told you this place was an Indian burial ground."

Dead Navajos, wrapped in colorful shrouding, lay on scaffolds eight or ten feet off the ground. Fargo knew the bones were eventually buried in another secret location after all the flesh rotted away.

A chamois tobacco pouch had been tied to a scaffold so the departed soul could smoke in the afterlife. Booger reached out to snatch it.

"Stay your hand," Fargo snapped.

"Ain't you the *sensitive* son of a bitch?" Booger shot back sarcastically. But, perhaps remembering his recent promise to obey Fargo's every order, he left the pouch where it was.

"There's the savages," Deke announced as they neared the spring. "Damn my eyes, lookit! They've butchered out one of their mules!"

"I couldn't stop him," Cherokee Bob said as the new arrivals lit down. "When All Behind Him gets hungry, he'll kill any man who stops him from eating."

"Never mind," Fargo said. "If things go our way, he'll have a horse to ride and plenty more to eat."

A little spring of clear, cool water filled a natural rock sink. Fargo joined the others and drank his fill before plunging his head under. Each man briefly dipped his weapons to cool them off, then reloaded.

"Bitch," he said, his voice all business, "we don't have much time. Hobble all the mounts after they drink."

He turned to Deke. "Did you divide that red chili powder into two sacks like I told you?"

"Sure. They're in my saddlebags, but what—"

"Caulk up." Fargo pointed back toward the entrance trail. "See those two niches on either side of the trail—the ones in shadow about twenty feet above it? There's staircase ledges leading up to both of them. When we finish here, I want you and Bitch to each take a sack and climb up on both sides."

Fargo untied his bandanna and handed it to Deke. "Booger, give yours to Bitch. Tie them over your nose and mouth. Wait until you hear the blast of Cherokee Bob's hand cannon. Then shake that powder out. Keep your eyes shut or it'll blind you."

"Fargo," Booger said, "you're the big bushway here. But I think your wick is flickering. Sure, Deke and Bitch ain't no great shakes as marksmen, but why waste two more shooters? They can't aim to shoot once that chili-pep powder gets to blowin' all around up there."

"There's no point in stuffing the hog through its asshole," Fargo said. "In warfare you have to mislead, mystify, and surprise your enemy. We'll call this one a surprise."

Fargo hated to stake human lives—especially his own—on one roll of the dice. But he had seen those highly trained and disciplined Spanish marksmen in action, and given their numbers, simply trading bullets with them was a fool's mission.

Fargo looked at the Delaware, who was contentedly mashing up a mule steak, his mouth ringed with grease.

"All Behind Him, I want you to haul that fat ass of yours up the entrance trail—quick. 'Bout halfway up you'll see a deep cleft in the rock, big enough to wedge back into. Once Deke and Bitch shake that powder out, horses and riders are likely to panic. They'll try to turn back. Use that pepperbox of yours and kill enough horses to choke the trail, y'unnerstan'? We want them forced out into the canyon."

Reluctantly, All Behind Him interrupted his chewing. "I do it. But take food."

"Of course. Hell, I can't ask a man to kill on an empty stomach," Fargo barbed. All Behind Him nodded in solemn agreement. Fargo shook his head in disbelief.

"Booger," he said, "me and you got the long guns, and Bob's a good shot with a handgun. It'll be up to us three to ventilate the Spaniards when they break out onto the canyon floor. Mister, I mean stack 'em up like cordwood."

Fargo looked at each man in turn. "Everybody understand what to do?"

They all nodded, Booger grinning like a proud tutor as he finally understood Fargo's plan.

Deke's Adam's apple bobbed nervously when he swallowed. "I understand, Skye. But it all gives me belly flies."

"Well, don't stand there gawking like a ninny. If you get nervous up there, count your toes."

Fargo jacked a round into the Henry's chamber. "All right, boys, let's get a wiggle on! They'll be on us quick, and we're gonna settle their hash for good."

19

Half an hour passed in tense silence. The only sound in the deep, empty canyon was the ghostly moaning of wind slicing through the narrow entrance.

Fargo, Booger, and Cherokee Bob fanned out behind granite boulders, eyes trained on the spot where the trace debouched into Diablo Canyon.

"Hell," Cherokee Bob called to Fargo and Booger. "You think maybe those stupid yacks rode on past?"

"They're out there," Fargo said confidently. "Salazar's a military man—he'll send a man in on foot to probe the entrance and get the lay of the place. Just hold your powder until I give the hail."

Sure enough, about ten minutes later Fargo spotted a face peering out into the canyon. The horses and Ambrose were in full view, but no Americans.

After about two minutes the face disappeared.

"Get ready to open the ball," Fargo told his companions.

Soon Fargo heard the snuffling of horses, the clinking of bit rings, and the creaking of saddle leather. And then Diego Salazar emerged on his magnificent Arabian black.

"Put at him, Bob!" Fargo called out, and suddenly the mausoleum quiet of Diablo Canyon was shattered by an ear-piercing blast that ricocheted back and forth between the high stone walls.

The distance was too great, and Cherokee Bob's smoothbore gun too inaccurate, to score a hit on Salazar. But the two-ounce ball punched into the Arabian's chest; its knees came unhinged and the black dropped dead in its tracks.

Salazar showed remarkable agility as he leaped nimbly

off his falling mount and dashed for the cover of a boulder. Fargo managed to get off a snapshot but missed, the round whining as it ricocheted off stone.

The detonation of Cherokee Bob's hand cannon had unleashed chaos on the narrow trace. Right on cue Deke and McDade had flung their ground red pepper onto the attacking troops.

The abrasive powder worked better than Fargo's wildest hopes. He glimpsed horses stumbling and rebelling, many throwing their confused riders. The soldiers, too, were temporarily blinded by the "devil dust," as Deke had taken to calling it. This terrible powder drove all courage and fighting spirit from a man instantly.

Fargo could hear those in the rear shouting the retreat, but All Behind Him's rotating-barrel pistol was chattering now, clogging the trail with dead horses. With no avenue left for escape, the only option for avoiding the swirling powder was the canyon itself.

Aragon, riding out front with Salazar, had missed the worst effects of the devil dust. He spurred his mount forward, a ridiculous sight as he waved his saber.

"Adelante!" he screamed, his face and voice fear-sharpened to the very edge of panic. "Forward!"

Fargo sighted down the long barrel of his Henry and squeezed off a round, the butt-plate thumping his shoulder socket. His bullet destroyed Aragon's left eye and drove into his brain. He slumped dead over his pommel as his panicked mount raced out into the canyon, ironclad hooves skittering on the smooth stone floor.

"Hot *damn*, Fargo!" Booger shouted over. "You sure can aim that smoke pole!"

But the discipline, courage, and marksmanship of these fanatical soldiers now had to be reckoned with. The roiling confusion of coughing, choking, blinded men began to take shape in a coherent defense as Diego Salazar, safe behind a boulder, shouted orders. Fargo could also hear Rivera bellowing commands but had not yet spotted the man.

The Spanish troops deserted their mounts and went to cover as a steadily increasing fire forced Fargo, Booger, and

Cherokee Bob to cover down. The shrill whine of ricocheting lead stayed constant, the thirty-shot lever-action Volcanics cracking ceaselessly now.

Fargo's Henry and Booger's North & Savage returned fire more sporadically, both men shooting only when men popped into view to fire on the Americans. Rock dust flew into Fargo's eyes, and one near-fatal bullet knocked his hat off and literally parted his hair.

Fargo heard Cherokee Bob cussing like a stable sergeant.

"It's you and Booger now," he called over to Fargo. "The firing pin in my damn handgun just cracked, and I'm out of balls for my cannon."

Fargo estimated there were at least a dozen soldiers still in the fight counting Salazar and Rivera. Deke, McDade, and All Behind Him were too far back to help and couldn't move from cover under the vigilant eyes of these sharpshooters.

Salazar now remained mysteriously quiet. Rivera, realizing the battle had reached a stalemate, suddenly decided on a coup de main.

"Forward!" he bellowed. "Kill them!"

Loosing a fierce battle cry, the Spanish soldiers rose from cover and surged forward toward Fargo and Booger's positions.

"Booger!" Fargo shouted. "Just like at Antelope Wells!"

Booger understood immediately. Several years earlier he and Fargo had been similarly rushed by a superior force of Comanches.

Both men rolled out from cover but remained prone. Booger started at the right end of the charging line, Fargo at the left, and they worked toward the middle. Bullets blurred the air around them, but the veteran frontiersmen focused methodically on one man at a time.

But these savvy troops did not offer themselves as easy, pop-up targets. They ran zigzagging avoidance patterns, tucked low, and rolled, even turned sideways when charging to reduce the killing zones Fargo and Booger were desperately seeking.

Fargo emptied his Henry, Booger his North & Savage, and both men went to their short guns in a blur of speed. Then the hammer of Booger's Dragoon pistol fell on an empty chamber just as Fargo slapped the spare cylinder into his own Colt.

During this frenzy of activity, Sergeant Rivera had managed to slip around to the right of Booger's position. Something glinted in the corner of Fargo's right eye. He swiveled his head to the right and spotted Rivera's wild-eyed face as he charged Booger from the flank, his deadly machete raised.

But Booger had spotted him, too. In an amazing display of speed and dexterity for such a big man, he leaped up, caught River's right arm, and twisted it hard until he dislocated the shoulder. Rivera screamed at the excruciating pain and dropped the machete. Booger caught it in midair.

A moment later, Rivera's severed head rolled and bounced toward the attacking men, now down to four. The headless body tried to deny the fact of death for several seconds, taking a few staggering steps even as blood fountained from the severed stump of the neck.

By the time it collapsed, all four of the attackers had been shocked immobile by the ghastly, unreal sight. With that unexpected hesitation they signed their own death warrants—Fargo rose to his knees, fanned his hammer, and sent them to fry everlasting.

"Fargo! Hold your fire!"

Diego Salazar stepped into view and tossed his rifle and sidearm down, sliding his sword from its scabbard.

"They are all defeated except for me," he said in his stiff, formal way. "But you gave me your word I would have the opportunity to settle a personal matter with you. This battle today involved the destiny of nations—but your filthy, despicable seduction of an innocent young girl is a personal affront to my honor and manhood. I demand that you answer for it."

An innocent young girl . . . If Fargo hadn't been so flabbergasted at this pompous fool, he would have laughed.

"Salazar, I knew you were an asshole the first time I met you," Fargo replied. "You deliberately stayed out of this battle so you could make that pretty speech just now. But you're right—I promised you we'd hug. So let's get thrashing. Booger, you and Bob stay out of this."

"I am the one who was wronged, so I will select the weapon. You can use Aragon's sword."

"Fargo," Booger muttered, "just shoot him. He knows gee from haw when it comes to killing with that cheese knife. I heard Rivera brag to Deke how Salazar won a trophy three years straight at that fancy Espanish college."

"Tell you what," Fargo told Salazar. "You use your blade and I'll use mine."

Salazar's wire-tight mouth curled into a sneer when Fargo raised his right foot and snatched the Arkansas toothpick from its boot sheath. But in just a few minutes Fargo would realize, too late, that he should have listened to Booger.

"It is your foolish choice, Fargo. I am going to watch your eyes lose their vitality as I drive the point of my blade into your warm and beating heart."

Salazar moved in at a glide, tossing his saber deftly from hand to hand. His skill in handling it was almost hypnotic.

"You're a damn good juggler," Fargo said.

Striking quick as a rattlesnake, Salazar lunged forward and slashed, ripping Fargo's buckskin shirt open. He followed up with a series of lunging slashes that forced Fargo to dance for his life.

"If you had a God, Fargo, you could beg him to receive you now!"

Once, twice, a third time . . . thirty-three inches of deadly Toledo steel, honed razor sharp, flashed past Fargo, and each time he barely managed to duck out of harm's way. With the fourth slash, however, he was not quite agile enough—hot pain licked his right arm as Salazar's blade bit into it.

"I cut you, Fargo. Feel it? Only a small taste of what is coming."

"Yeah, but you made one mistake—you didn't kill me."

"Mistakes can be rectified."

Fargo had desperately been working to get in close to Salazar with his knife. But when the Spaniard's blade cut his arm, and Fargo ducked back out of the way, Salazar lunged even closer.

Fargo felt a tug at his waist, and a moment later his trousers nearly fell. Cursing and stumbling as Salazar roared with laughter, he was forced to use his left hand to hold up his trousers.

Booger had reloaded and now raised his pistol.

"Don't do it!" Fargo ordered. "He gets his chance to kill me fair and square."

Again, again, and yet again, Salazar's deadly blade came within a hair of slicing Fargo. Backing away from yet another wild flurry of slashes, Fargo suddenly tripped on a rock and went down hard on his ass. Salazar was on him like dark on night, his cruel, handsome face glowing with triumph as he prepared to make the *paso de muerte*.

Fargo felt a leaden heaviness in his stomach and barely managed to hop backward, crab fashion. He felt the wind from Salazar's saber as it flashed past his head so close it sliced off a hank of hair.

Fargo realized how much he had underrated the Spaniard. The man's balance was sure as a mountain goat's, his movements quick as a cat's. Fargo was still too busy scuttling out of the way to get his trousers untangled and stand up.

As Salazar drew back for yet another thrust, his dark, goading eyes met Fargo's. They blazed like hellfire, and for one chilling moment Fargo was sure he had finally met up with Old Scratch himself. Salazar deftly flipped his wrist, the blade flicked quick as a whip, and Fargo again scuttled nimbly backward—but not quite far enough. Fiery pain made him grunt as the filigreed blade opened up a cut on his chest, the second wound in less than thirty seconds.

"You know what, Sancho?" Fargo taunted, seeing that Salazar was nearly overcome with emotion—and thus susceptible to mistakes. "I pounded the spike maul to Miranda so hard I had her barking like a dog. I had to shove a pillow over her face, she came so loud. And by the way, she's got a snatch like a tight velvet glove."

A red film of uncontrollable rage replaced Salazar's eyes, and he finally did what Fargo had been hoping he would—he stepped in too close.

Fargo wrapped both legs around Salazar's left leg and rolled hard to the right, throwing the man crashing to the ground. Before the Spaniard could recover, Fargo twisted around on top of him and drove the Arkansas toothpick deep into his entrails—so deep he felt heat wash over his hand.

Salazar's high-pitched scream almost made Fargo forgive

157

him for the two wounds, it was so hideous—especially when Fargo made a point of twisting his blade hard, both ways.

"That's called the Spanish twist," Fargo informed the dying man. "Kind of ironic, huh?"

Fargo heaved himself to his feet and planted one foot on Salazar's chest, tugging his knife back out. The two wounds were giving him jip, but neither one was deep.

Cherokee Bob caught his eyes. "You know, Fargo, I wonder."

"Wonder what?"

Bob nodded toward the dead man. "If All Behind Him would be interested in eating that son of a bitch. He likes Spanish food."

20

Fargo slapped alum powder on his wounds and wrapped them with linen strips. The first unpleasant task, after the battle in Diablo Canyon, was tossing finishing shots into the wounded Spanish soldiers and horses. This was standard practice for Fargo ever since a possum player had nearly killed him in Arkansas.

"You two," Fargo told Deke Lafferty and Bitch Creek McDade, "are both a credit to your dams. For tenderfoots, you hung in there like hairs in a biscuit. Without the help of that devil dust, we'd all be cold as a basement floor."

Deke puffed his scrawny chest out like the cock of the dung heap. "No need to coddle *me*. I wasn't a-scairt."

Booger made a farting noise with his lips. "Hell, your part in it was small bore. You boys wanna see a sight that'll tear your hearts out?"

He turned around to reveal a bullet hole in the seat of his pants. "Ricochet got me right in the ass. I'm leaving the slug in as a souvenir."

Cherokee Bob and All Behind Him ignored the others, busy robbing the corpses. McDade glanced around nervously at the dead bodies.

"This is an Indian funeral ground. What happens when they find all these dead Spaniards littering their sacred ground?"

"Let's just say we don't want to be here when they do," Fargo replied.

He pointed to a gutta-percha water bag tied to the saddle horn of a dead horse. "There's a few more of those. Let's make sure we fill them before we ride out."

"I wunner where the viceroy and the two women are waiting," Booger said.

"Yeah. We've got a little problem there—Quintana. He's the head of the snake, but how are we gonna prove it?"

"You ask me," Deke said, "he needs to have a little accident."

"Given his plan," Fargo agreed, "that just might have to happen. I hate to play it that way, though. Don't forget there're others in on this shindig. I'd prefer to have proof."

The second unpleasant task was using ropes and elbow grease to haul out several dead horses clogging the trail. Booger's prodigious strength helped immensely. The horses that had not been killed escaped into the surrounding desert as soon as the entrance was cleared.

They had just begun the seventy-mile ride back to Las Cruces when Fargo reined in. About a quarter mile ahead, a gray gelding, saddled and hobbled, was standing with its head down in the oppressive heat.

"There's a man lying near that horse," Fargo said. "And judging from that fancy frock coat, I'd say our problem with Hernando Quintana has been solved."

They gigged their mounts forward and confirmed the body was indeed Quintana's—a silver-inlaid, ivory-gripped "muff gun" lay near his outstretched right hand.

"Why, he closed his own account!" Booger exclaimed. "Shot an air shaft through his head."

"Looks like maybe he rode in with the rest," Fargo speculated, "and waited here for the good news. But he must've recognized Salazar's death cry, and when none of his men rode out he figured out what happened."

Fargo squatted on his heels and searched the old man. He found a thick sheaf of papers in the inside breast pocket and quickly perused them. "Boys, we've struck a lode. Here's all the battle plans and a bunch of letters about it from somebody in Sacramento named Augustine Sandoval. Bob, they're in Spanish. I'll sound them out and you help translate."

According to the letters, Quintana was hauling a hundred and fifty thousand dollars in silver bars to pay and equip a military force. Their plan was to seize the arsenal at Benicia and then the capital in Sacramento.

Booger whistled. "A hunnert and fifty thousand! Boys, that'll make a nice split for us—we sure's hell earned it."

"Nix on that," Fargo said. "The moment you smell mustard you start crying roast beef. Unless that money was stolen, it belongs to his only heir—Miranda."

"Well, he's sure got a fine watch," Cherokee Bob said, unfastening it from Quintana's vest.

Booger shot him a murderous look. "Who you gonna say this one belonged to—Ben Franklin?"

"Don't let his daughter see any of that loot," Fargo admonished, knowing he'd never get it back from the Shawnee without killing him.

"We just leaving the body here?" McDade said when Fargo crammed the papers into a saddle pocket and forked leather.

"That's my policy," Fargo replied. "I'll bury anybody except a man who tried to kill me. Let the buzzards feast. One of you boys tie a lead line to the gray before All Behind Him butchers it out."

With plenty of water and the cooler night air, the riders made good time. Exhaustion finally settled in around midnight and they slept beside the trail for four hours, riding into Las Cruces about an hour after sunrise.

They left their mounts at the livery and discovered the Quintana party conveyances still parked behind the big livery barn. Fargo washed up at the stone trough and changed into his spare buckskins. Then the six famished men visited the La Paloma Café and devoured a huge breakfast of eggs and the spiced sausage called chorizo.

Fargo inquired at the front desk of the Montezuma House and learned that Miranda and Katrina had been allowed to keep their room. He next faced the unwelcome task of telling Miranda her father was dead by his own hand. He produced the sheaf of papers and Katrina translated them for Miranda while Fargo improved on the crease in his hat.

"Skye," Miranda said, looking up at him where he stood gazing out a window, "was my father buried?"

"He was," Fargo lied shamelessly. He added a postscript: "We buried all of his possessions with him. It was a lonely grave in the desert, and we figured you'd want him to have them."

"Yes. He especially cherished his watch."

Fargo looked solemn. "I noticed it was a nice one," he said, figuring Cherokee Bob was probably already trying to sell it.

"Katrina and I knew he was up to something," she said. "But *this*—why, it's treason! He was an American citizen. And this one letter from Sandoval—it makes it clear that my father intended to give me to Diego Salazar as payment if Diego led a successful military action. My own father!"

"The world isn't likely to grow honest anytime soon," Fargo said awkwardly. He wasn't much good at consolation.

"Well, he was my father, and of course I love him. But for that very reason I also despise him. Suicide was at least an honorable choice."

Katrina seemed less sympathetic. "He knew he would be executed anyway, Miranda. The government takes a very dim view of treason."

Katrina looked at Fargo. "You killed *all* of the men?"

"We had no choice. They were fanatics loyal to Spain and this plot, and it was us or them. They couldn't let any of us live."

"This silver," Miranda said. "It is my father's entire fortune. I knew it was hidden in the coach, but I had no idea what he intended to use it for. Will the government confiscate it?"

"They won't because they aren't going to know about it. Only one letter mentions it, and you're going to lose that one. But we have to make sure this Augustine Sandoval is jugged and the plot broken up. I know the army judge advocate up at Fort Union. I'm sending him a telegram today and asking him to send a courier down to pick up these papers."

A smile ousted Miranda's frown. "Katrina and I can't tell you how *grateful* we are."

Fargo felt a stirring in his loins. Few things were more pleasant than a grateful woman—or two.

"Just one question, ladies—do we finish this journey to California?"

"Neither one of us ever wanted to go," Miranda assured

him. "We don't know one soul in California. Our entire lives are centered on New Orleans, or at least mime is. I was born there, all my friends are there, and Katrina has lived there for ten years. We wish we could go back."

"All right, then, you will. But we'll need Booger, Deke, McDade, even those two lazy, conniving Indians to get it done. Are we all hired?"

"Of course. No one ever fired you. Skye?"

Her voice had grown husky in a way Fargo recognized. "Yeah?"

"Do you realize there will be no one preventing you from . . . visiting us in the tent on the way back?"

"The thought has crossed my mind more than once," he admitted.

Katrina spoke up, giving him a sultry up-and-under look. "Do we *have* to wait until we leave? Why don't you lock the door for a while?"

Fargo felt a grin tugging at his lips and sudden pressure in his hip pocket.

"Yeah," he agreed, crossing toward the door. "Why don't I?"

LOOKING FORWARD!
The following is the opening
section of the next novel in the exciting
Trailsman **series from Signet:**

TRAILSMAN #385
THUNDERHEAD TRAIL

*1861, in what will one day be Montana—where a bounty is
being offered for a killer with horns.*

Skye Fargo wasn't surprised to find a town where there
hadn't been one two years ago. New towns sprang up all the
time. This one had a single dusty street and barely twenty
buildings, but one of them was a saloon.

A crudely scrawled sign Fargo had passed not a hundred
yards back said the town was called Trap Door. It seemed a
strange choice, but when it came to naming towns, people
could be downright peculiar. There was a town he'd stumbled
on once called Sludge. The name he liked the most was one
he heard about from back east. It was called Intercourse.

He figured naming a town Trap Door was someone's
notion of a joke.

He didn't know what to think of the naked woman standing in the middle of the street.

Fargo drew rein to study what he was seeing. Fargo, a big
man, broad of shoulder and hard with muscle, wore buckskins and a white hat so dusty, it was brown. A Colt was on

his hip, and unknown to anyone else, an Arkansas toothpick was strapped to his leg inside his left boot. Women rated him handsome. Men rated him dangerous.

The woman in the street was in her twenties or so.

Long brown hair fell past her bare shoulders. Her head was down and Fargo couldn't see her face. He did see that she was quaking as if with fear. Her arms were across her breasts and she stood with her legs half-crossed.

Fargo looked up the main street and then down it and was further surprised to find there wasn't another living soul in sight.

Just the naked woman and no one else.

Fargo gigged the Ovaro, and when the stallion was next to her, he drew rein again and leaned on his saddle horn. He was tempted to say, "Nice tits," but he decided to be polite and said, "How do you do, ma'am?"

She didn't look up. All she did was go on quaking.

Leaning on his saddle horn, Fargo said, "Folks don't wear clothes in these parts?"

Her hair was over her face, and when she raised her head just a little, a single green eye peered out at him.

"You shouldn't," she said.

"How's that, ma'am?" Fargo said while admiring the rest of her.

"You shouldn't talk to me," she said, her voice trembling like she was. "It's not safe."

"Safe for who?"

"You, mister. He won't like it. He'll hurt you or worse. Or his brothers will."

Fargo looked around again. Horses were at hitch rails and a cat was licking itself but they were the only signs of life. "Where is everybody?"

"Hiding."

"From who?"

"Mister, please," she said, practically pleading. "Ride on before it's too late."

"I was thinking of wetting my whistle." Fargo hadn't had a drink in a week and a whiskey would go down smooth.

"God, no. You don't want to. Light a shuck before one of them looks out and sees us."

Just then there was a loud crash from the saloon and a burst of gruff laughter.

The woman nearly jumped out of her skin. She quaked harder and balled her hands, her fingernails biting into her palms.

"You have a name?"

"Just go. Please."

Fargo bent down and carefully parted her hair with a finger. She didn't try to stop him. He spread it wide so he could see her face, and a ripple of fury passed through him.

Her left eye was fine but the right eye was swollen half-shut. Her right cheek was swollen to twice its size and was turning black and blue, and blood had trickled from the corner of her mouth and dried on her chin. Someone had clouted her, clouted her good.

"Well, now," Fargo said.

"Please," she said again.

"How long have you been standing here?"

"I don't rightly know. An hour, I suppose. Ever since they rode in and he got mad at me for not wanting to sit on his lap."

"I need a handle," Fargo said.

"Folks call him Grizz on account of that's what he looks like. Him and his two brothers show up from time to time to have a frolic, as they call it."

"How about your own?"

"It's Candice." She glanced over her shoulder at the saloon. "God, you're taking an awful chance. For the last time, please skedaddle or they're liable to do you harm."

"Where did your clothes get to?"

Candice looked down at herself and closed her good eye and a tear trickled from it. "Grizz ripped them off me after he hit me and I was lying on the floor. He said how he'd teach me to mind him and told me to come out here and stand until he hollered for me to come back."

"Well, now," Fargo said again. "I reckon I'll have that drink." He raised his reins but she clutched at his leg.

"I'm begging you. Go before it's too late. I don't want you stomped or killed on my account."

"You say he has two brothers with him?"

Candice nodded. "Rance and Kyler. They're almost as snake-mean as Grizz. Rance carries a Sharps everywhere and Kyler is partial to a big knife. You don't want to rile either of them. Both will kill a man as soon as look at him."

"You don't say."

She removed her hand. "Now that you know, fan the breeze."

Fargo clucked to the Ovaro and made for the hitch rail.

"Wait," Candice said. "Where are you going?"

"To do some riling," Fargo said.